GARDEN IN HEAVEN

Stories, Poems and Dreams

Josephine Whyte

Copyright © 2022 Josephine Whyte
This book is sold subject to the condition that it shall not, by way of trade or otherwise, be lent, resold, hired out, or otherwise circulated without the publisher's prior consent in any form of binding or cover other than that in which it is published and without a similar condition including this condition being imposed on the subsequent publisher.
The moral right of Josephine Whyte has been asserted.
ISBN: 9798365605046

This is a work of fiction. Names, characters, businesses, organisations, places, events and incidents either are the product of the author's imagination or are used fictitiously. Any resemblance to actual persons, living or dead, events, or locales is entirely coincidental.

For J
I kept my promise
You knew I would
- G

CONTENTS

Grandma Clementine *1*
First Day *4*
The Inner Child *6*
Picnic in the Park *9*
Invisible Friends *11*
She's Only a Baby *13*
Seashells *16*
Wind Chimes *19*
The Auld Yin's Perspective *22*
A New Beginning *25*
Calls to Agony Aunt Maureen *29*
The Handcuff Charade *35*
Stories From the Photograph Box *39*
The Promise *44*
Ewan's Tooth Extraction *51*
Snowflakes *55*
We Are Going Camping *61*
But For How Long? *61*
Lily's Friends *65*
Artist's Dreams *72*
Eavesdropping *76*
Dreams of Italy *82*
The White Feather *86*
The Northern Lights *92*
The School Uniform Shenanigans *99*
Intangible *105*
Enchanted Woods *109*
The Young Un's Perspective *112*
Hide-and-Seek *120*

A Scottish Miners' Gala 128
from a Child's Perspective 128
Mischievous Angel 133
I Wanted to Run but She Made Me Crawl 135
A Cool Time 142
Our Day 148

Grandma Clementine

Ruth stood staring unseeingly out of the bay windows. Normally, she felt the tension leave her body when she looked out at the rolling green fields and the shimmering sea where the sky and land seemed merged together, but today, the pain of losing her grandma was overwhelming. She felt an aching loneliness engulf her. She sighed, brushed her short blonde hair back from her face in agitation and, with shaking hands, lit another cigarette.

James, her twin brother, sat in a Queen Anne chair (which Grandma loved because it was so ugly) and looked sadly at Ruth. They had both loved Grandma Clementine deeply and hadn't realised how much they depended on her until now. James took a gulp of whisky. Apart from the soft sound of the white flimsy fabric of the window curtain blowing gently in a soft breeze and the sound of birds twittering, there was absolute silence in the room.

"Isn't it funny how the world keeps ticking on no matter how you feel? The birds still sing and life keeps trundling along."

James knew Ruth wasn't looking for an answer. Even today, after Grandma's funeral, he smiled a little half-smile to himself; if anyone knew Ruthie, it was him and Grandma.

He sat sipping whisky. Not his favourite tipple, but Grandma always kept a full decanter on her dressing table and today seemed as good a day as any to numb himself. He looked at Ruth silently. Brother and sister held a strong sibling love for each other, but in looks, they were completely different. James was dark-haired, short in stature and prone to putting on weight easily, whereas Ruth was blonde, blue-eyed and slender to the point of thinness.

Suddenly, Ruth let out a scream and pointed a finger at the large photograph of Grandma that sat on the dressing table. James jumped up, spilling his drink and shouted frantically, "Ruthie, are you okay?! Oh God, what's wrong?"

Ruth stared at the photograph and whispered, "Grandma winked at me, James. She winked at me."

James stared at the photograph and after several seconds, said crossly, "Just shut up, Ruthie. This is no time for going loopy on me. Come on, we're the only sane ones here. Grandma's relatives downstairs are the nut jobs, not us."

Ruth picked up the photograph and held it, tears rolling down her face, "She winked at me James," she said almost reverently. "I'm not making it up."

Slowly, they sat down together on the white silk sheets of the antique bed and stared at the photograph.

It was a favourite of Grandma's. It was taken on one of those rare, precious days that stay locked in your memory. They had gone to a country park for a day's outing. The weather had been warm, almost balmy for late September, the sun glinting through tall trees of every description. The three of them had sat on a picnic rug drinking champagne (Grandma's treat) and enjoying thick slices of rye bread dipped in olive oil and a selection of various cheeses and hams, with juicy peaches and beer to wash it all down. How they had laughed. Silly conversations and jokes totally in tune with one another. As they had packed up to go home, Grandma had held them and kissed them tenderly on their cheeks, saying it was the most cherished day of her life. Then, Jamie had taken a snapshot of Grandma's face, her wrinkled blue eyes laughing up at the sun, her thin-veined hand on top of her white sun bonnet as if an invisible wind was going to blow it away. She looked serenely happy.

"This is how she would want us to remember her," James said softly. "The good times we had together and how we promised her we would look after each other."

"She did wink at me, I promise!" said Ruth emphatically.

"You know what, big sis? I believe you."

And then, to his own astonishment, James thought, *I really do.*

First Day

Shona's hands trembled slightly as she ran them through her short brown hair and tried to tell her reflection in the full-length mirror that she really could do the job or she wouldn't have been chosen. Anyway, people always said that the first day is always the worst. But it didn't matter how much she tried this so-called psychoanalysis; it just wasn't working.

Then, the phone rang. Its piercing shrillness broke into Shona's conscious fears and she knew, she just knew, exactly who that would be.

And it was.

It was her elder sister Anna. As much as they loved each other, lately, Shona was beginning to face the fact that Anna was happier if Shona was in her "little box", a box Anna had created for her, and God help her if she tried to step out of it. Shona had been reflecting on her past life a lot recently and these thoughts seemed to be coming up more frequently. For example, one time, she had excitedly showed Anna her graduation ceremony photos and Anna had just dismissed them with a flick of the wrist and immediately changed the subject. Shona had even sifted through all the graduation cards her friends had sent her, pointing out her favourite ones, but Anna airily dismissed them all with, "Didn't seem to me like you tried that hard."

Another time, she had been about to go out for a coffee with a friend. Just then, Anna had phoned to say that their elderly father needed company and she was too busy running the family business to attend to him, so Shona would have to do it.

How many years has this been going on? Shona thought to herself. *The manipulation, the eroding of confidence and self-esteem. Why did I allow myself to placate and please her?*

With determination, Shona looked in the mirror once again and thought, *I can do this*, took a deep breath and walked out of the door to her first day at her new job.

Behind her, the phone continued to ring.

The Inner Child

I sit amongst the trees, watching the sun drying the diamonds of dew on the grass. Only the chatter of birdsong breaks the silence. I am listening to a child's laughter and the sound of footsteps crunching on the gravel as a man and the child walk along the leafy path which separates the trees in the woods. They walk this way most summer mornings. *Ah, here they are – I can see them*, I think excitedly as I run through the woods to walk with them.

I know they cannot see me, but sometimes I think they feel my presence – a caress on the cheek, a wisp of a soft, strange breeze blowing in their hair.

As I walk with them, I look at the tall, lean, handsome dark-haired man dressed in old working clothes. Although he looks to be in his early thirties, his face is tired and drawn today, but it lights up with a big, beaming smile as he listens to the child's incessant chattering.

The child is around four years old and I can't help but smile – she is utterly enchanting. Her chubby little legs and freckled face are brown from the sun. Her long ringlets catch the sun's rays, turning her hair into the colours of falling autumn leaves. She is dressed immaculately in a short, bright blue sundress that perfectly matches the aquamarine colour of the sky. She skips along the path, holding his hand and in her other hand, she carries a tiny, bright red plastic bucket filled with the wild rose petals she has just picked. Every so often, she will drop a few petals on the path. When the man asks her why, she tells him, "It's just like the Hansel and Gretel book you read to me. If we get lost, we will just look for the petals and find our way home." He smiles down at her childish innocence.

She vainly tries to take huge steps to keep up with his long strides, but after a short while, she gives an exaggerated yawn, saying she's tired and needs to be carried on his shoulders. He laughs down at her and says, "No, we have just started walking. Our day has hardly begun. I will carry you when I know you really are tired." The child gives in with good grace. I smile because she asks her dad the same question every morning and always gets the same answer.

The old church gate creaks as they enter the grounds. Acres of overgrown fields surround the white-painted church. *This man has much work to do*, I think. He begins to work and all that can be heard is the swish of his scythe and the child singing lullabies as her dad continues to cut the grass, with one eye on the child. She sits down on the newly cut grass and becomes completely engrossed in making daisy chains, chewing her bottom lip in concentration as her tiny hands clumsily try to pull the daisies together. He sits down beside her and pulls a packet of Love Hearts, her favourite sweets, out of his deep trouser pocket. She lets out a whoop of glee and sucks at the sweets contentedly. He takes a cigarette from behind his ear and lights it as she finally succeeds in putting the daisy chain haphazardly around his neck. The sun is hot and as she looks up at the cloudless sky, she holds up her sticky hands and begins to dance, delighting in her day.

As the sun begins to cast shadows that lengthen, the child falls asleep, her face hot and sticky from the sweets. The man lifts her gently and begins to walk through the fields towards home. I walk beside them and watch the inner child that was me.

To the memory of my dad. I miss your wisdom.

Picnic in the Park

Lottie hobbled painfully towards the playground. The arthritis in her legs was throbbing worse today than yesterday. *Funny how old age creeps up on you,* she thought. She knew she was old. Her aching bones, poor eyesight and failing hearing told her so, but sometimes, she still felt like a young thing of eighteen. Then, by God, she'd catch a glimpse of herself in the mirror and she would damn near die of fright and ask herself, *Is that old crow looking back in the mirror really me?*

Lottie chuckled to herself. It didn't seem that long ago that she was young and sprightly. She and Jamie used to dance around their tiny "butt and ben" cottage to their favourite Glenn Miller songs, getting slowly inebriated on whatever concoction Jamie had tried his hand at this time.

He was so handsome, her Jamie, and he would always be looking out for her, she thought wistfully.

Although God had decided in his mercy and wisdom, and at this thought she frowned with disdain, to take him to a better place, even after all these years, the emptiness sometimes enveloped her in unguarded moments.

God had blessed them in many ways, but not with bairns.

She made a habit of feeding the ducks in the park on fine days, but really, it was to watch the bairns play and laugh at the mischief the bonny wee things got up to.

"Life happens when you're busy making other plans," Lottie whispered to herself. "But bairns, oh aye, they have the ability to live only in the present and to enjoy every second of it."

Having manoeuvred herself onto a bench, Lottie observed the young mums talking and laughing, but with their eyes constantly watching their children.

One of the young mums shouted, "Hiya Lottie, how are your legs today?"

"Not too bad, hen," Lottie breathlessly shouted back.

The young mum shouted again, "We're having a picnic here tomorrow around noon, would you like to join us, Lottie?"

"I'll be there, hen. Noon's just dandy," Lottie shouted back. Lottie's heart soared; she had been invited into their little group! She hugged herself with glee.

She drew herself up slowly, reaching for her walking stick, and began making her way home. She'd make her own special clootie dumpling for the picnic. Jamie's face had always lit up when she'd made him clootie dumpling, she remembered fondly.

Suddenly, she had a fleeting thought that filled her with dismay. *Perhaps they know I don't come to feed the ducks but for the enjoyment of watching the bairns.* She dismissed the thought immediately. After all, she had a busy evening ahead of her and was so looking forward to tomorrow.

Invisible Friends

Two tiny fairy cousins, Annabelle and Petula, sat close together, dipping their feet in a stream, surrounded by a sea of bluebells which, in the fairy world, meant that they were surrounded by love and protection.

They laughed, their voices tinkling in the gentle summer breeze and, if heard by those not of the fairy world, it would sound like the whisper of trees swaying ever so softly on a hot summer's day.

Looking at them, one could be forgiven for thinking they weren't related. Annabelle, the slightly older of the two, had a mass of tumbling red hair and piercing blue eyes, whilst Petula had short blonde hair and brown eyes, and was of a quiet and placid nature, not prone to the temper tantrums of her cousin.

They both yawned sleepily, agreeing that they were tired – it had been an exhausting day searching to and fro for flowers to make daisy chains for their fairy friends, but their task was done and it had, after all, been such happy day.

Although only seven years old in the fairy world, they talked of the conflicts witnessed in the human world and humanity's greed and cruelty.

They shook their heads sorrowfully, remembering the times they had happily played with human children, but as the children grew older, they no longer believed in their "imaginary" friends.

Annabelle shook her head again and said, "Petula, the adults tell the children we do not exist and when this belief is instilled in them, they no longer see us. The adults have taken us away from them. In the adult world, Petula, it is frowned upon to have imagination."

"That is why, Petula," Annabelle explained, "We in the fairy world have to keep hidden from the human world."

Annabelle angrily splashed her feet in the stream, causing sprays of water to cascade upon Petula, whose bottom lip was trembling slightly at Annabelle's words.

Seeing Petula upset, Annabelle slipped her hand into her cousin's and said, "Come, Petula. Let's go and play in the fairy ring with our fairy friends."

And with that, they skipped happily through the woods.

In memory of my mum, for believing in me. This short story is the first one I wrote for her.

She's Only a Baby

I crawl around in my playpen, laughing, whining, gurgling and crying. The world believes that because I am a baby, I cannot understand. But I understand much more than you all know.

My family are under the illusion that as long as I am fed, have my nappies changed and am given love and attention, I am happy. But I see the world through knowing eyes, as all babies do.

I love my mum and dad and know that they love me too. But sometimes, I hear them arguing about the long hours Dad works, how exhausted Mum is and whose turn it is to look after me when I cry during the night.

I have unconditional love for my only sister, Ally. She is around eight years old, has long blond hair and big blue eyes. Oh, how I love to grab those long plaits when I think she is not giving me enough attention! When she comes in from school, she kisses and cuddles me close. I particularly like her tickling my toes and when I start to laugh, her face lights up and she will shout for my mum saying, "Oh mum, look at her laugh!" Though she didn't find it funny when I laughed so much that I was sick all over her school uniform. She actually shouted at me in disgust. Mum was really angry with her and said words like, "For goodness' sake Ally, she's just a baby! What else do you expect when you tickle her so much?"

When mum puts me in my playpen, there is a huge mobile hanging above my head. It seems to me like it's full of dangling teddy bears, stars and horses, and when mum winds a key at the back of the mobile, the baby music plays. I like my mobile. When I listen to the music, it lulls me to sleep and helps me forget that my mouth is sore from my first tooth coming through. However, I like it even more when I am taken to look outside through a window. Ally takes my index finger and points to the falling snow, the thousands of twinkling stars in the dark night and tells me stories about all the adventures we will have together. That is my special time with Ally.

Mum tries hard to give me attention but I know she is busy. She's a dressmaker by trade and most of the time, she sits at her sewing machine and to be honest, the whining noise it makes drives me mad.

Mum's friends sometimes come round for coffee. When they do, they start cooing and saying how big I've grown. It really annoys me, especially when I'm sleeping and they wake me up. One of mum's friends wears this horrible-smelling perfume and I've learned to wrinkle my face in disgust and start screaming. It's the only way to stop her picking me up. One day, she actually said to mum, "May, I don't think she likes me very much."

Mum cheerily answered, "Don't be silly Mavis, she's only a baby!"

But if I could talk, I would agree with Mavis.

Daddy comes home from work, cuddles me close and whispers sweet nothings in my ear, and if I give him a big, watery kiss, his face lights up even if his face and shirt are covered in my dribble. Well, I can't help that I've just started teething.

I like being taken for walks in the pushchair to look at the ducks floating in the lake, but I'm really quite scared of big dogs and those jet planes which fly fast, really low and make a huge noise. One day, I was so terrified, Mum had to take me home and cuddle me for what seemed to be hours. In the end, I was quite happy to be put in my playpen.

Oh, if only the world knew how much we babies really know about you.

Seashells

Diane walked slowly down the pebbled path, finally arriving on the beach. She had tied her long auburn hair into a careless ponytail and wore a pair of yellow shorts and a bright green T-shirt. She was thankful that she had had the foresight to dress for today's hot weather. As she slipped off her old leather sandals, she muttered to herself that she must get a new pair sometime soon. Diane's friends would laugh knowingly at this, as "sometime soon" would be at least five years away. She sighed, running the warm golden sand between her fingers. She felt tired and was looking forward to a day when all she had to do was sit and look at the sea. She took an old yellow and grey blanket from her basket and sat down. Although it was September, the beach was practically deserted. *Mind you, it's school time,* she thought. Funny how you forget dates and times. Now that her boys had left home and were happily getting on with their own lives, she couldn't remember when school holidays began and ended.

After looking for a while at the tranquil colours of the shimmering sea, a mixture of green and aquamarine, she decided to go for a walk along the shoreline. Squinting against the hot sun, she gave such a loud gasp that any onlooker would have looked at her in amazement. She had just glimpsed the most beautiful shell lying in the sand. It was partly covered by driftwood, but she caught sight of the glistening light which reflected off of the shell. It was beautiful; silver and dusky pink, with shades of the palest lilac and green. *Just like the ocean on a summer's day*, she thought as she picked it up.

She returned to her blanket and gazed at the shell, almost mesmerised, and for a few minutes, held it in her hand. Then, in a child-like way, she held it to her ear. That's when memories, long forgotten, came rushing back.

Memories of herself and her son Aaron, dressed in summer clothes. She was wearing a white shirt, pink shorts and sandals and holding Aaron's hand tightly. *He must have been just around three or four years old*, she thought. He was dressed in a blue top, navy shorts and blue wellingtons, which he had insisted on wearing despite the summer heat because he wanted to play with the fish in the sea. She laughed to herself at that memory. He must have looked ridiculous, but she hadn't cared. They were going to have such a happy day.

They had collected seashells together in his white plastic bucket. He was shouting with excitement at everything he was witnessing, whether it was the shape of the clouds in the sky, the colours of the sea, the little pools of water beside them, or the small boats far away on the horizon. He had such fun from a child's perspective, finding the world such a total joy to be living in.

She remembered his gurgling laughter so vividly, and his shining eyes, the colour of melted dark chocolate, as they played with the seashells. His clumsy little hands seemed to her to take ages to painstakingly take the seashells out of his tiny bucket but finally, he managed it and together, they held the shells to their ears, listening. Diane remembered saying in a soft voice to Aaron, "Keep the shells close to your ears, shut your eyes and believe me, whatever you hear, you will see."

Diane could see Aaron was concentrating hard, as only children know how to, his little hands clutching the shells to his ears as he whispered back, "I hear seals, Mum. Guess what? The seals are playing all around me."

She had also brought bubbles for him to play with on the beach and as he blew, Diane remembered trying to catch them. "You've missed that one, Mum," he had laughed out loud, his little face beaming with happiness and laughing so much that the few people on the beach turned and smiled at him.

The seashells were put aside, he had wanted to build a castle. Then, he splashed around with the waves coming in to the shore, shouting excitedly, "I won't get wet, I've got my wellies on!"

When his dad came to collect them to take them both home, Aaron insisted on taking the bucket full of shells with him and spent the next few weeks holding a shell against each ear and saying excitedly, "I'm listening to the waves, I'm listening to the sea and I see the seals."

Wind Chimes

Sylvia sat in a garden chair, her chin cupped in her right hand as she looked at the blue velvet sky, where thousands of stars twinkled. It was a warm, balmy night in September, unusual for Scotland, and she was revelling in it, sitting in shorts, a shirt and sandals. *Long may it last,* she thought, knowing full well that this wonderful weather would be fleeting.

The house was in darkness. Only the kitchen lamp was visible from outside. Under normal circumstances, she was really afraid of the dark and could barely sit outside by herself. When Ned, her husband, would announce that he was going to bed, she always stayed inside the house. She would imagine a dangerous stranger lurking behind the garden trees or in the bushes, waiting for a chance to pounce on her, not to mention those big, wild cats that supposedly roamed the forests and woods. Mind you, and she laughed softly to herself, her mam had always said she had a vivid imagination. But tonight, she wasn't afraid. In fact, she was relaxed and thoroughly enjoying herself. She had tried to hide her fear of the dark when the two boys were children, and she liked to pretend to herself that she had succeeded. She had always believed that whatever fears you have, you pass on to your children. She had tried hard not to do that.

Tonight, however, she had no fear. It was all because of the wind chimes which Ned had hung on top of the swing at the end of the garden. Sylvia was mesmerised by them. A small glass ball, with four long, oblong wooden pipes surrounding it and at the bottom of the ball, a metallic butterfly. When it was dark, the ball changed colour from bright azure blue, to jade green and finally, a bright crimson red. The colours changed every minute or so and the wooden pipes chimed, a gentle tinkling in the breeze.

Beth, her sister, knew her fear of the dark so well. *God bless her,* Sylvia thought lovingly. Beth had given her the wind chimes to try and overcome her fear of the dark and it was actually working.

She no longer felt the garden to be such a frightening place at night. Random thoughts began to pop into her head, like how it was funny that she didn't really like gardening, whereas Ned loved it. He was never happier than when pottering around planting seeds, herbs and flowers. Sylvia consoled herself with the thought that Ned loved to plant them but she actually liked to watch them grow. In a strange way, she thought the plants were like children. *If you nurture them and talk to them, they will grow,* she mused. "God, I'm going barmy," she said out loud to the garden, laughing softly.

She realised she could probably sit here until dawn came, enjoying the ever-changing colours and sounds of her wind chimes and the peace of the dark stillness.

She didn't often have time to just sit quietly and think, but thanks to the wind chimes, maybe, just maybe, she would do it more often.

The Auld Yin's Perspective

"Has Granda done a bunk again, Mam? That auld yin is living the life of Reilly since he moved in with us – gallivanting here, there and everywhere," said Rory. Sarah's sixteen-year-old son grinned cheekily at her as his right arm lurched across the kitchen table to grab the packet of Coco Pops, narrowly missing a carton of milk which he had left precariously balanced on the edge of the table. If he had spilled it, she would have been the one down on her hands and knees cleaning up the mess. With Rory, any time she asked him to do anything his reply was, "In a minute, Mam." However, that minute never seemed to materialise.

God help us if this is an example of our future generation. She smiled inwardly at where her thoughts were going, but she tried to look sternly at Rory and said, "That's enough cheek out of you, young man. Taking the mickey out of your granddad like that! I won't stand for it. He's worked hard all his life. It's his time to enjoy himself and if he chooses to spend it at the bookies or in the pub, that's his business. So don't you go and start winding him up when he comes home."

Rory laughed and Sarah said sternly, meaning it now, "I'm warning you Rory. And anyway, just exactly how many bowls of cereal have you really eaten today? This packet is just about finished and I only bought it yesterday. You young ones think money grows on trees."

"Och, come on Mam, lighten up," Rory said chirpily. "I'm an expert at winding you up too, but I'm starting to think Granda's got a bit on the side these days, what with his wandering off, telling no one where he's going. You know, last night, he even asked if he could borrow that expensive aftershave you bought me for Christmas. I was gobsmacked."

Rory was now almost doubled up with laughter. Sarah tried to playfully swipe him with the kitchen towel as he ran upstairs, no doubt to either sleep half the day or play endless computer games. *This so-called school study leave is a joke*, thought Sarah crossly. She had yet to see Rory study anything more than the latest computer magazine.

At that moment, Sarah's dad walked in with a big cheerful grin and handed Sarah a box of chocolates, Cadbury's Roses; her favourites. "Here," he said, "these are for you. I won fifty pounds at the bookies, so I treated my mates to a round of drinks at the pub and I've a wee present for Rory. Where is he anyway?"

"Supposedly studying upstairs," Sarah replied irritably.

Sarah's dad looked intently at her for a few moments and then quietly said, "I know he can be an untidy, cheeky wee blighter Sarah, but he's never given us any real cause for concern. He's a good laddie. Think of the worry other families have to live with. I mean, look at your pal Pat's laddie Jason, the company he keeps, his drug-taking, the police knocking at her door every other week." He shook his head and said, "That poor woman must be demented."

Sarah gave him a quick cuddle and they both started to laugh as they heard a voice bellowing from the top of the stairs, "Is that the auld yin back from his gallivanting?"

A New Beginning

Rosie's tired and deeply wrinkled face was flushed with excitement. Her faded blue eyes lit up as she counted out, for what she considered the umpteenth time, the two hundred pounds she had won at the bingo earlier this evening.

Tomorrow, she promised herself, she would treat her new friends to a fish and chip shop tea, and it wouldn't be just their usual order. Naw, it would be what they called "aff the fancy menus", wi' all the trappings that came wi' it. Soft slices of brown and white bread wi' lashings of butter and mushy peas washed down wi' mugs of tea so strong that they would often have a laugh, saying that they could have a wee dance on top of it.

She hobbled towards her favourite armchair in her tiny, cosy living room, looking around it with pride. Her gaze lingered fondly over her wee knickknacks, reminders of her and Joe's life together.

Talking out loud, Rosie said, "Ach it's grand, so it is, to be at ma ain fireside." Rosie liked to talk out loud to herself because she firmly believed that Joe was avidly listening to every word she uttered.

When Joe, her husband and best friend, had died, their home, which was once filled with so much love and laughter, was simply no longer home to Rosie anymore. All of a sudden, it became a frightening and extremely lonely place to be in.

Although it had taken time to adjust to a different way of life, she was relieved that she had finally summoned up the courage to move into sheltered housing accommodation.

She had the best of both worlds now, she thought. If she felt in need of company, she would go to the large communal dining room, where there was usually someone to share a blether and cup of tea with. And if she wanted privacy, she could stay cocooned in her flat and find contentment in her own wee world. "Aye, Joe would be happy for me," Rosie murmured, taking a gulp of coffee from a mug heavily laced with whisky and smiling contentedly.

Joe, knowing how fond Rosie was of her Irish coffees, would make up a large one for her and, handing it to her, would say, "Right, ma wee lamb, you'll sleep nay bother tonight once you've got that down you." It was a nightly ritual, down to the same words being spoken each time.

Adding another generous dash of whisky to her coffee, she lovingly fingered her wedding ring, seemingly unaware of just how deeply it was cutting into the swollen joints of her finger.

She then proceeded to tell Joe about her "wee adventure" the previous day at the local hospital's out-patient department. "Ach Joe, ah was only going to get this auld leg of mine checked oot and it was when that young whippersnapper in a white coat," at this, she paused for a moment and sniffed disdainfully, "Suggested that he would now proceed to cut aff ma wedding ring as ma finger was swollen." She now shook her head vigorously, "I screeched at him, Cut aff ma wedding – ma wedding ring?! Have you taken leave of your senses, boy?! You bloody young eejit. Barely out of nappies and nay doubt still tied to your mammy's apron strings. You young uns wi' your fancy certificates think you know it all but you know nowt up here. Joe put this ring on ma finger over sixty years ago and by God if ma Joe was here today, he would skelp your lugs so he would. You young uns have nay respect for us auld yins and if ah had the strength ad kelp you maself.' At first, Joe, he looked at me like I'd grown two horns." Rosie started to smirk, thoroughly enjoying relating her wee saga.

"He looked horrified when ah tried to grab ma walking stick to clobber him wi' it. Ah was then kindly escorted aff the premises by those two security guards that I know quite well and whom I have to say, Joe, are perfect gentlemen."

A sudden thought occurred to her and she frowned, puzzled. Didn't one of the security guards say, "See you next time you have an appointment, Mrs Robertson." and the other security guard muttered words to the effect that the next time she had an appointment he was changing his shift because he was heartily sick to the back teeth of having to be sweetness and light when escorting auld biddies off the premises when all he really wanted to do was put his two hands around the old bag's scrawny neck and throttle her?

Rosie shook her head and muttered, "Naw, it wouldny been me he was talking about. Must be another auld biddie who had obviously been giving those two lovely gentlemen a terrible time of it."

She lifted her hand to look at the thin gold band gleaming in the light of the softly glowing lamp and said smugly, "Aye Joe, but ah came home wi' ma wedding ring firmly intact."

Calls to Agony Aunt Maureen

Her grandchildren had all clubbed together to buy her a computer. "It will be really cool, Granny," her granddaughter Jenny had said. "Something to give you an interest and tide you over in the winter months when you're snowed in."

"In this god forsaken cottage at the back of beyond," she had added in an undertone, putting another log on the fire and shivering as she did so. Marjory had looked at Jenny, thinking affectionately that these young uns had no stamina, with all their central heating and fancy gadgets. When she was growing up, you just had to get up out of your bed in the freezing cold and run hell for leather to the brightly lit coal fire in the living room. She had fought with her two sisters to see who could get closest to the crackling flames.

At first, Marjory had been totally frustrated trying to get to grips with the computer. She actually thought her old-fangled brain throbbed from concentrating, and her arthritic fingers were stiff after jabbing at the keyboard for what seemed like hours. A few times, she was sorely tempted to fling the damned thing out of the window and tell the grandchildren her house had been burgled and whoever it was had taken the computer with them, but perseverance prevailed. Gradually, she began to get the hang of it and then, low and behold! While browsing through the Internet, she came across an advert for a local agony aunt in her small town. It was only for 30 minutes a week, but she was sure she wouldn't just be good at it, she would be brilliant!

She painstakingly filled in the application form, adding and deleting pieces she thought were either none of their business or, in her eyes, irrelevant. "After all," she said tutting, "what exactly did they mean by in your prime?"

"Clever", "articulate" – well, that was definitely her. She knew that folk in the small town where she lived thought she was a bit odd, but she thought of herself as eccentric, and never dim-witted.

Surprisingly, after a fleeting interview on the phone, she was offered the job. She didn't want the town folk to know her real identity, so she had changed her name from Marjory to Maureen. She was actually nervous, realising that she would soon be talking to her first caller over the Internet, but these people had problems, and no matter how big or small, it was up of her to help them out.

And so, the calls began.

The first caller was a woman called Pat. "I know I'm a just an old fool Maureen, but I had a one-night stand with an old fling and I think I might be pregnant."

"What age are you, love?"

"57 on my last birthday."

Poor soul, thought Maureen sympathetically, *she must be a bit dim-witted*. "Now," Maureen said firmly, "you're way past your sell by date in that department, my love. Now don't be taking offence," as she heard a gasp on the Internet. "Take my youngest, Debs. She can't pass a man on the stairs or she's up the spout. Don't let him be taking advantage of you, will you?"

Pat gave out a huge laugh and said, "Taking advantage of me? That's one for the books! I was wined and dined, had a brilliant time afterwards, if you get my drift, and now I've got him eating out of my hand."

"Okay then, Pat. It's your life. Let me know how it goes."

"Hi Maureen, it's Leslie here. Just need a wee bit of advice."

Maureen thought Leslie's voice sounded a bit wobbly but said, "Fire away, I'll give you what advice I can."

"Well," the caller's voice grew even more wobbly. "Me and my Tim have been married for over forty years, and you know what he got me for my birthday?"

"A romantic holiday somewhere exotic?" Maureen exclaimed enthusiastically, immediately thinking what a stupid remark that was to make. If it had been a lovely holiday, she would hardly be asking for advice, would she?

"No," Leslie said tearfully. "A new ironing board."

"New ironing board?" Maureen repeated. "By God, I'm not usually stuck for words but I'm absolutely gob-smacked. Are you stuck for cash?"

"No," Leslie replied, still sounding tearful.

"Do you have a joint account?" Maureen asked hopefully.

"Yes," Leslie answered, hiccupping.

"Then get right down to the bank, draw out a huge

amount, phone up your best friend and tell her you're taking her on a wonderful holiday. Then straight down to the travel agents, book somewhere warm and sunny and when you go home, you tell him where he can stick the ironing board. Give him the shock of his life, he will never treat you like a doormat again, I promise you."

"Thanks Maureen. I'm off right now."

"Mind you don't let him back you out of this. He has got his just desserts, so he has."

The next call was from a tearful Diane. "Maureen, I've just had a massive argument with my husband. We've only been married a month and I think I love my dog more than him."

"Was it over a serious issue?" Maureen asked with concern.

"Not really. He just went to the pub, had one too many and was sick all over the bathroom floor."

"You made him clean it up?" Maureen asked sternly.

"Of course I did," Diane replied crossly. "What do you take me for, a total eejit?"

Mollified, Maureen said, "You will love him again when you've decided to make him suffer just a wee bit longer, but in my humble opinion, you can get rid of a man but not your dog. I should know, I've been married four times and would rather have had my dogs any time. Trouble with dogs, dearie, unless they are prize winners at shows or are directly linked to her Majesty's corgis, they don't bring in any money. So let him suffer a bit longer, keep your chin up and let me know how it goes. I wouldn't be one bit surprised if he's planning to cook you a slap-up meal tonight."

"Thanks Maureen, I feel so much better. Bye."

"Hi Maureen. My sixteen-year-old laddie is in agony with toothache and I cannot persuade him to go to the dentist. You would think I was sending him to the Gestapo the way he's carrying on. To be honest with you, I think he would rather get blind drunk, give one of his mates a pair of pliers and tell them to get on with it. You know what gave him this fear? I think it was him watching that Dustin Hoffman film, the Marathon Man, I think it's called. You know, the one where he's getting all his teeth pulled out."

"Now you listen to me dearie. Pay more attention to what your laddie is watching. These television programmes have got a lot of responsibility on their shoulders, just look at all those gambling adverts for a start. Don't they realize many people are actually addicted to gambling, or is it they want to make so much money from poor unfortunate folk they just don't care with the mess of today's society? Far less some of the rubbish on the Internet. You tell him, if my laddie can go to the dentist, anybody can. Dentists are not the horror stories they are made out to be, it's like when my Debs was having a baby. By God, the horror stories she would tell me that her so-called mates told her, I felt like wringing their necks, so I did."

"And another point, you're getting yourself in a bit of a tizzy, if you don't mind my saying so. He's hardly going to let one of his mates come near him with a pair of pliers after watching the Marathon Man, is he?"

"Aye, you're correct Maureen, I'm exaggerating."

"Be firm with him, but a wee bit of friendly advice here: Pick up the phone on the fly, give the dentist's surgery a quick ring to let them know how petrified he is – they will have heard it all a million times. I can promise you, waiting rooms in dentists' surgeries are full of terrified people. Don't allow him to go on his own in case he does a runner for the hills. Let me know how it goes and explain to him how good he will feel once he's had his treatment. No more pain. The dentists are there to help him."

"I will, Maureen. Thanks," Irene said gratefully.

"That was the last caller until next week."

Marjory was tired, but she also felt invigorated and so proud of her accomplishments today. She sat in her old armchair watching the blue, orange and yellow flames dancing amongst the crackling logs, hoping she had helped the callers. She knew diplomacy wasn't her middle name and with Marjory, what you see is what you get. Well, she would find out next week if any of those who had talked to her today would get in touch with her again. *It feels good to be useful again*, she thought with a satisfied smile.

The Handcuff Charade

Olive sat in the supermarket café, thoroughly disgruntled. This was the second pair of school trousers she had had to buy her seven-year-old son Logan in a month. *It's never ending,* she thought. *Well, that's another pair been bought – until next week, no doubt.* It was a myth that kids grew out of their clothes so fast; Logan was never in clothes long enough to grow out of anything.

Still, after the money she had spent on that wee devil, she actually had some left over. The sales at the supermarket were still on, so she had managed to get his trousers half price. She deserved a well-earned rest and bought herself a bacon roll and a huge mug of coffee. She opened up the pages of her library book and was just about to start reading when two women came and sat at the next table…

Now, Olive would never consider herself to be a nosy person. She called herself an observant non-participant, if you know what I mean, but although she pretended she was engrossed in her book, she was actually listening to every word they were saying.

One of the women looked to be in her late forties, with

short auburn hair, dressed in jeans, trainers and a pink top that Olive much admired. Her friend, whom Olive thought was probably in her early seventies, had white hair cut to perfection and heavily jewelled rings on each finger. She had pink manicured nails and was extremely well dressed in grey trousers, a short black jacket and black short boots. Olive thought to herself, *God, compared to her I feel even more of a frump than I usually do – now I am really fed up with myself.*

"Linda," said the older woman loudly, "It's coming to the stage where I dread coming to the supermarket. The price of everything seems to increase every week."

"I know, Helen," Linda said, frowning. "But with this recession, it's not going to get any better, so why don't we just switch off for a wee while because I want to give you a really good laugh about last night's shenanigans."

Helen was all ears and said laughingly to Linda, "Oh God, you didn't get drunk and make a fool out of yourself again, did you?" Linda indignantly replied, "No, I certainly was not drinking. Even if I had wanted to, I couldn't after that total horror of a son of mine did what he did to me."

"And which son would that be?" Helen said, laughing. "The quiet one or the wee imp?"

"Who do you think?" Linda asked humorously.

Linda continued, "You know how I hate ironing, Helen?" Helen nodded knowingly. "Well," Linda said indignantly, "I tried really hard to get him ready for his new police training session. I spent a whole hour on his police trousers and guess what?" She looked horrified, as if she had just been struck by lightning. "He came last in his class at the inspection – last! Can you believe it? I half killed myself to make sure he was

God personified. When I got his phone call, I was shocked. Shocked, I tell you."

By this time, Olive was already spluttering into her coffee, but Linda was continuing with the saga. "After all that, the wee imp waltzes in with all his police paraphernalia, you know, the baton and yellow jacket so bright it just about made me go blind, and then his lordship asks quite cheerfully, "Mum want to have a go with the handcuffs?" Of course I was feeling guilty about him coming last in his uniform parade, so I played along. I tell you Helen, when he put those handcuffs on me it was a wee bit painful. Helen nodded dutifully, not having a clue what Linda meant but trying to be sympathetic all the same. "Well," Linda continued, "you will never believe what that wee imp did."

"Come on then, Linda, tell me. I can't wait to hear this one," Helen said, laughing.

"He went away with the key and I was left sitting in the armchair, handcuffed. I couldn't even lift a cup of tea, far less a gin and tonic."

"After about ten minutes, but what seemed like hours to me, Tom came back from playing bowls. 'Get these handcuffs off me now – right now!' I said, and you know, Helen, he just looked at me and talked to me like I was a five-year-old and said, smirking, 'Linda, these handcuffs are not the cheap plastic stuff we bought the boys for Christmas when they were young. These are real handcuffs, only the police can take them off'."

"I had to sit there all night long until that wee imp came home from having a night out with his mates and waltzed into the house. I let out a roar, 'Where the hell have you been?' With those big, blue innocent eyes he said, 'I've been out for a few pints, Mum, have you been missing your wee fags?' Naturally, I wanted to thump him, but couldn't because of the handcuffs and then he said, 'Och Mum, calm down'."

"God, if anything causes me to go ballistic, it's the words 'calm down'. Then he said, 'I have a few phone calls to make, then I'll get my key and release you'." At this point, Helen started laughing. "I remember that song – it was that Engelbert Humperdinck – 'Please release me, let me go'."

Linda looked at her coldly, she didn't find it funny, but by then, Olive was laughing so much she choked on her roll.

Helen turned round, looked at her in concern and asked, "Are you all right, love?"

At this point, Olive was laughing so much she had to leave her bacon roll and coffee and make a beeline for the toilets. Her trying shopping trip was totally forgotten, and the day seemed a lot brighter.

Stories From the Photograph Box

Gayle shivered despite her warm, green winter jacket. The wind was blowing fiercely as she hurried through the cobbled streets towards May's flat, thinking it was more like November than August. May was sitting at the living room window, obviously watching for her. Gayle waved cheerily. May waved back as she rose to let Gayle into her little flat. Gayle kissed her fondly on the cheek and thought, *God, I love her. She always makes an effort to put on one of her posh frocks for me*, and felt guilty for even imagining cancelling tonight because she had so much work to do at home.

Tonight, May was dressed in a black velvet dress and, of course, her pearl necklace and earrings. Her white hair had obviously just recently been permed by Pam, the local hairdresser, who came every week to make sure May's hair was just as she liked it. Gayle knew that as hard as May might have tried to get her swollen arthritic feet into a pair of shoes, she hadn't been able to manage, so as usual, she had her old, comfortable slippers on.

They sat together as they did every Wednesday night: May in her old chair with Gayle kneeling beside her. As usual, May had laid out her best china cups, saucers and small plates. Gayle poured the tea. May had insisted on making the tea herself this week, as she had given Gayle the tiniest wee bit of a row last week, saying, "Your tea tastes like water, I like tea I can dance on." After May had finished dunking her favourite shortbread biscuits into her tea, thoroughly enjoying every mouthful, they began their weekly ritual.

The ancient shoe box sat on top of a small table. Gayle picked up the box and gently placed it in May's lap. With her old, paper-thin wrinkled hands, May began to take out the old photographs.

Gayle knew that May's old photographs meant the world to her and together, they slowly went through them. They were black and white pictures, grainy with age, of May's late husband Jon and their two sons, who must both be nearly sixty years old now, Gayle surmised.

May always told different stories about how her two sons Jack and Tim were so different in nature but had always stayed so close. "Jack was a wee devil," May said, lovingly stroking the photograph. "Look at him, Gayle," she chuckled. "The laughs he gave myself and his dad and, by God, he just egged Tim on. When Tim would say 'No – I hate football', Jack would tell him to stop being such a wimp and you know who ended up in hospital with his leg broken? Well, it wasn't Jack – it was Tim."

May was laughing now, wiping the tears from her watery old eyes. "By God, Gayle, they two were a pair. Look at them – like butter wouldn't melt in their mouths. A pair of wee angels." From the photograph, Gayle could see exactly where she was coming from, except for the cheeky grin on Jack's face. The boys were a year apart in age and identically dressed in white shirts, black shorts and black plastic sandals. Jack had curly blond hair and a beaming smile, while his wee brother, standing timidly behind him like a startled deer, had dark hair and dark eyes. It was obvious who was the instigator between the two.

"The time Tim got caught for stealing apples from that posh chap's orchard down the road, Jack had managed to get over the wall, but poor Tim was too slow, crying all over the place because he'd been shouted at by the man who owned the place. He called the police, who drove Tim home. I think even the policeman felt sorry for him. He had his arm around him as he brought him up the garden path. I couldn't be angry with him, he was in such a state. 'Oh Mam, I'm so sorry', he had sobbed. The way he carried on you would have thought he had murdered somebody and of course, by that time, Jack had legged it home and was lying in bed pretending to myself and his dad that he was reading a book. When I went upstairs to ask where he had been that day, I saw the book. He had never read a book in his natural life and then, when I saw it was an encyclopaedia, I knew Jack was behind it all. And all Jack was concerned about was that Tim had got a lift home in a police car and he hadn't, and I just said to him, 'Well, you shouldn't have left your wee brother alone, should you?'"

"God hen, I could talk about those two all night; chalk and cheese, but they were good for each other, not bad laddies," and she looked at me with wisdom in her eyes and said knowingly, "We did an a'right job bringing that pair up. After all, they still call women ladies."

"Aye, I remember the time they were about six and seven. They went away to the wee cemetery on their old bikes and rearranged all the flowers, taking from the graves of those who had plenty and putting them on the graves of those who didn't, just to ensure everybody was equal." She laughed at this. "A few of the folk in the village who had just laid the flowers weren't too pleased, but then they thought it was funny when they knew the laddies had meant no harm. Then the next thing I know, the parish priest was at my door to say they had been drinking the holy water from the fonts on their way back home. Their explanation was that they were just thirsty and knew God would understand."

"And shortly afterwards, Jack persuaded Tim to climb up to the top of a tree in the woods. Jack got bored, climbed down, lay on the grass and fell asleep. Tim was stuck up there for an hour, hollering for Jack to help him down and it was my old friend passing by who had to climb up to get Tim down while Jack was fast asleep. When he got the telling-off of his life from myself and his dad, he just innocently said, 'Mam, I'd had a hard day fixing all the flowers in the graveyard and was knackered, if I'd heard him, I would have helped him down.'"

She took out the photographs of her two wee angels at Christmas, "You know lass, they went down to the living room during the night in the early hours of Christmas morning, squabbling over what present one had got and the other hadn't, so they decided to come to an amicable agreement and exchange certain presents. No doubt they had a good laugh together, thinking myself and their dad would be none the wiser. The next morning, we had to pretend we hadn't noticed. Aye, the stories I could tell you lass, but they will keep for next week."

"Aye, those were the days, those were the days," May murmured to herself as she retreated into her own wee world. Gayle could see May was tiring now. She lifted the photographs to put back into the box, but not before May had told her exactly in what order they were to be placed. Gayle laughed indulgently and said, "I know May, I know."

May was falling asleep. Gayle washed up the china dishes and put them on the kitchen dresser saying, "I'll see you next week."

To which May drowsily replied, "Aye, but before you go, put on my favourite video for me. James Stewart, 'It's a wonderful life'. Always loved that film."

Gayle dutifully did so. Then, covering May in a warm fleece blanket, she softly kissed her goodbye.

A last word from May on the way out the front door, "See you next week lass, and mind you don't forget my shortbread. Aye, you're a good lass, you've never forgotten your old neighbour."

Gayle laughed to herself as she made her way home. Aye, there was only one May in this world, that was for sure.

The Promise

Sue gave an enormous sigh and shuffled uncomfortably on the train station seat, vowing to herself that she would not look at the time on her mobile phone yet again. She was harassed and in a thoroughly bad mood, and her sister Caroline wasn't exactly a bundle of laughs either. When some woman smiled at them sympathetically, it took all of her willpower to give a half smile back.

Their godmother, Maud, was coming to Edinburgh before she continued with her holiday in the north of Scotland. She had decided to pay them a visit, which they were both dreading. In Maud's words, "One must carry out one's duty. Therefore, I am duty bound to pay you both a quick visit," which had been delivered in her brisk, no-nonsense voice devoid of all emotion. And so, they had turned up to meet her and, no doubt, to go on to a hideously expensive restaurant dating back to the 1950's that Maud always liked. A place where time had stood still, with the owners and workforce looking down their snooty noses at people like her and Caroline.

"Oh, God, the old bat's coming within range – I can feel the vibes," Caroline said frantically, clutching Sue's arm. Sue rubbed her pinched arm angrily and said, "Will you get a grip, Caroline. She's got a nasty tongue in her head but we're no longer children. Just smile like you're a halfwit and before you know it, she will be away to some ancient hotel in the Highlands, making other people's lives a misery. We won't have to meet her again for a while."

"October 29th, that's when we meet her again," Caroline whispered. Incredulously, Sue looked at her and said, "Don't be so intimidated by her. She's nasty and bitter, but deep down she's really unhappy."

"The rays from your halo are blinding me," Caroline said sarcastically.

Both sisters watched as Maud strode along the platform, barking out instructions to whoever she had found to deal with her insurmountable luggage. If only she had some respect for others, but for as long as the sisters had known her, she had always bullied people, and there was not much chance of that stopping now. In fact, as she grew older, she became more intolerable.

They had often wondered how their parents, now both dead as a result of a car accident, had time and patience for Maud, but Caroline thought it was simply because they had more empathy in their big toes than she and Sue would ever have.

"I do feel sad for her," Caroline commented. "But not enough to be the lashing post for her cruel tongue and vicious put-me-downs regardless of whose listening. She just doesn't give a damn."

The sisters watched Maud approach. She was tall and thin, with her black hair severely tied in a bun and, needless to say, impeccably dressed in a green tweed skirt suit and black flat shoes, with a black designer bag firmly in her grasp. Her spectacles dangled from a gold chain round her neck. Her eyes, though faintly dim with age, were piercing all the same and bright red lipstick glistened on her thin lips. Her whole demeanour oozed aristocratic bearing, money, and God help anyone who did not behave as they should with her bearing down on them. She eyed each sister up and down in disapproval, obviously finding them deeply disappointing.

Her accent is the only soft thing about her, Caroline thought. It was a beautiful, lilting accent from the island of Lewis. *I bet the islanders had a massive "knees up" when she left*, she thought, laughing in her head at her own joke.

Maud's impeccably manicured red nails lifted her glasses and slowly put them on. She proceeded to air kiss them both and then said, "Well, you two never change, do you? What kind of dress sense do either of you have? Caroline, you really do need to get some professional weight loss guidance and as for you, Susan, you look like you've been dragged through a hedge backwards. Where do you go to get a hair style like that – a sawmill?"

"Och well, still the same godmother who endows us with endless self-worth and leaves us overflowing with confidence," Caroline said testily as they made their way after Maud.

"I think she's chosen to ignore you," Sue giggled, mimicking Maud's walk and soon, they were laughing out loud. Maud turned round, telling them in no uncertain terms to stop behaving so childishly and get a move on.

The evening meal at the expensive restaurant was dismal. Class distinction and a servant-master attitude still prevailed beyond any doubt. With its old wooden panelling and high ceiling with a massive, protruding chandelier, the restaurant reminded Sue of old black and white films of dreadful boarding school assembly rooms. There were numerous paintings of eerie country manors, horses and, worst of all, those stern, obese old men with thick rolls of fat around their necks – the type that were your worst nightmare if you happened to bump into one of them on your way home. Sue gave an involuntary shudder and Caroline winked knowingly at her.

Maud stated matter-of-factly that she had already ordered for them earlier. When Sue said she would prefer a pint of lager instead of wine, the silence in the room full of old, upper-class clientele seemed to go on forever. Maud completely ignored her.

Maud was not one to lose her temper. She considered herself too well bred for that, but there was just no holding her vicious tongue. She poured forth a stream of acidic criticisms, from their appearance to their lifestyle in general.

For the love of God, will she just not shut up, Sue thought, as she looked over at Caroline who had her head bent over her plate, picking at the food she was eating.

As Maud continued to belittle them, Caroline found herself no longer listening. She wondered why two adept, independent, capable women were prepared to sit here and listen as insult after insult was piled on them, just for the sake of their deceased parents' friendship with this woman. It was beyond any concept of rationality why they would ever want to associate themselves with this woman, far less allow her to be their godmother.

Caroline gathered her thoughts. Hadn't there been something between Maud and Dad's oldest brother? Weren't they supposed to get married but he had left her standing at the altar? Faint memories of one occasion when Mum, usually a placid soul, had been shouting at Dad, saying that she was demented with Maud latching on to them and making the girls' lives a misery. Dad replied with something like they were the only friends Maud had. Mum's scathing reply was that Dad's brother, Ewan, had left her because she had always been a nasty, evil piece of work who was only happy when she made those around her miserable and that she had had enough. Caroline recalled that nothing had changed after that, everything carried on as normal when Maud was around: Mum tight-lipped and silent, Dad doing his best to be the life and soul of the party.

She wondered briefly if Maud had something on Mum and Dad that she used against them. Perhaps she had paid off their debt and they felt they owed her. She could, come to think of it, remember a time when her parents seemed to fret constantly about their lack of money and then, all of a sudden, their financial problems had disappeared. Perhaps Maud had given them a loan or something and that's why she could bully them so ruthlessly and walk away without even a brief half apology. In fact, it used to take Mum days to recover after a visit and as for Dad, he had always been able to stand up to anyone, so why didn't he stand up to Maud? She gave herself a mental shake. Her imagination was starting to run riot, if she didn't watch out, she would end up as barmy as Maud.

Her daydreaming stopped as she really looked at Maud. She didn't see a lonely, sad woman but a woman who was hellbent on damaging people's lives, something that gave her greater satisfaction than all her piles of money ever would.

She then gazed at Sue's white, pinched face, the way in which her long, pink dress only accentuated her thinness, the slight tremor of her hands and her pale, pain-filled eyes. Her husband of five years had left her six months ago for some woman he'd met at a work conference and Sue was suffering terribly.

Maud was sitting there, a paragon of virtue, thoroughly enjoying herself. "Well, someone has to tell you, so I'm taking it upon myself to do just that."

I bet you are, Caroline thought viciously, but she still wasn't ready for the ensuing ruthless attack on Sue.

"Really, Susan, surely you must have realised that in order for you to keep a wealthy, professional man like Bryan, you would have to change your appearance, your personality – quite frankly, everything about you – in order to keep him. It was no surprise to me that he found someone more to his liking. You've never had much to contribute in any way, it was really just a matter of time. As I said to my friends, I'm honestly surprised he put up with the marriage for so long, it's not like you've ever had anything going for you, is it?" She paused as she calmly picked up the delicate glass of expensive, ruby-red wine and took a tiny sip.

At that moment, Caroline heard Sue give out a soft moan and she looked at the additional anguish, evident on Sue's face, that this woman had caused. Caroline had never felt such murderous, burning anger towards anyone and she knew never would again. With an icy-cold calmness, she slowly stood up. Sue had never seen her sister so angry and also stood up as Caroline, in a voice laced with venom, quietly said, "I truly believe you are the devil incarnate and on both my own and my sister's behalf, I promise you will never see either of one us again – ever."

Sue took Caroline's hand and together, they slowly walked out of the musty, claustrophobic room, surrounded by the shocked silence of the other diners.

Outside, the sun was shining. The street was full of people of all nationalities enjoying the good weather. Sue and Caroline hugged each other tightly. Caroline was shocked at how thin and fragile Sue felt, but then Sue smiled, her first genuine smile in such a long time and said, "I'm so proud of you. I feel like a weight has been lifted from my mind." For the first time, Caroline really believed that Sue was going to be fine – better than fine. She was going to be happy again.

"Let's go and have a well-deserved toast to us," Sue suggested cheerfully, and they both walked through the old, cobbled streets, arm in arm.

Ewan's Tooth Extraction

Moira sat on the living room sofa, having just handed her fourteen-year-old son Dean some cotton wool, on which she had dabbed small amounts of clove oil whilst looking distractedly out of the window at the watery sun. It had been a long night, she thought. She had been up most of the night due to Dean's toothache. She was tired; in fact, she was exhausted.

Her other son, Ewan, who was twenty years old, looked at Dean, seemingly unconcerned about his pain. "You eejit. You kept me up most of the night. I hardly slept a wink with you howling in pain and Mum running in to see you every couple of minutes like a demented banshee with every concoction in those stupid herbal books she reads. Well, let me tell you," he said, giving Dean a filthy look, "You're not the only one in pain. I'm knackered too."

Moira gave him a warning look. Ewan thought, *God, I'm in the firing line*, because he knew when Mum gave that look it could make hell freeze over. "Your breakfast is in the kitchen, Ewan," Moira said tersely. "I suggest you go and collect it." And with her tone of voice, Ewan knew exactly what was going to happen next.

He nonchalantly shrugged his shoulders, saying, as he removed himself from the living room sofa, "Well Dean, I don't have much sympathy for you. Mum's been telling you for years to get to a dentist and you just kept putting it off like you put everything off that you can't be bothered to deal with. That's your problem, you just don't listen to anyone, do you?" At this statement, Dean grunted and tried hard to kick Ewan, while still holding the piece of cotton wool in his mouth. Ewan laughingly said, "Missed! You're losing it pal, losing your touch."

Moira looked on in exasperation, although secretly thinking that if Dean could try to kick his brother, he wasn't in that much pain. She made her way into the kitchen to get Dean yet another drink.

She had managed to get him an emergency appointment at a dentist's for surgery that afternoon, and as Ewan swanned into the kitchen, she hissed, "You could show a bit more concern for your wee brother, he is in a lot of pain. The last thing he wants to hear any more of your wise cracks."

"Aye, I hear you mother," Ewan said sarcastically. "I've been listening to him howling like a dog all night and I'm knackered."

"For God's sake, Ewan, "Moira said impatiently. "You'd think you were ninety years old and not twenty."

"I need my beauty sleep," Ewan yawned, having a wee laugh to himself, knowing that he was winding her up.

"I will beauty sleep you right now," Moira snapped. "That's what you get for wandering in here at three in the morning after a night out with your mates. By the end of this day Ewan, you will be even more knackered, because guess what?"

At this, Ewan gave an exaggerated sigh, and asked, "What, Mum?"

Moira exasperatedly replied, "Dean is your wee brother and you are going to take him to the dentist and look after him properly, and I mean properly, Ewan. No pulling any stunts like going off to some pub for a quick pint while he is with the dentist. Have I made myself perfectly clear?"

"Aye, Mum," Ewan said wearily. "But the problem is, Mum, my mate Andy loaned me the latest computer game. He's been raving about it all week, and I can't wait to get started on it." To this, Moira dismissively retorted, "The game will wait. Your brother needs to get to the dentist, and I can't take him. I've got to go and check if your granddad has eaten his dinner. You will do what you are told Ewan; that's the end of it." Moira rummaged in her handbag, finding her purse and handing Ewan twenty pounds. "That's enough money to get yourselves a McDonald's cheeseburger or whatever, although I very much doubt poor Dean will be able to eat anything."

At the sight of the money, Ewan's face brightened up. "I hear you loud and clear Mum," he said, giving her a perfect mock salute, and muttered, "The Gestapo wouldn't have stood a chance if you had been against them in the war." He thought Moira hadn't heard him but she had and looked at him sternly.

"Now enough of your cheek, off you both go. I know you had planned your afternoon, Ewan, but let's face facts. My idea of utopia isn't exactly sitting in a dentist's chair, and you know Dean is terrified of going. Just make sure that when he has seen the dentist and had his treatment, you give me a call from your mobile immediately to tell me how he is. I'm counting on you."

"I know Mum. I'll look after him. He will be grand," sighed Ewan, resigning himself to the awful truth – he was in for a horrible afternoon.

Two hours later, Moira's phone rang. It was Ewan, and he was laughing. "Well Mum, I managed to get young, demented Dean to the dentist and I do feel rather sorry for him. He had to actually get his lower gum stitched. I left him at the bus terminal." When Moira started shouting at him, he held the phone away from his ear, lifted his eyes to the heavens and said, "No Mum, not to go for a fly pint, to get to a toilet, and when I came back, he said a tramp was going around trying to find fag doubts on the ground and was desperate to get Dean to talk to him. Of course, with Dean's mouth all stitched up, he was finding it difficult to talk to anybody, but he managed these words Mum: 'What a geek!'"

Moira said she would give Dean an earful for cheekily talking to anyone like that when he got home, but she secretly couldn't help laughing. The story would cheer her dad up to no end. He always enjoyed hearing about the antics the pair got up to.

Snowflakes

Bryony, dressed in a shabby but warm multi-coloured dressing gown and pink fluffy slippers, padded into her large ultra-modern kitchen and reached for the kettle, pushing her curly short brown hair out of her face. She rubbed her bleary eyes, still half asleep; her actions were on autopilot. The kitchen was always bright, but it seemed somehow brighter than usual this morning.

She looked towards the tall glass sliding door that ran the length of a wall opening up to the back garden and gasped in astonishment and delight; huge, fat snowflakes were falling heavily and silently. She walked over towards the glass wall, mug of tea in her hand, and plonked herself down and snuggled into the small sofa which was covered with soft squidgy cushions. This was her favourite place to sit in the house.

With her hand on her chin, her face broke into a huge smile. Anyone observing Bryony would at first glance acknowledge that she was one of those nondescript people – someone whose looks would not stand out in a crowd – but when she smiled, it was like a flower opening up in the bright light of the sun.

Beside her was an old wooden footstool which she had picked up from a car boot sale and had lovingly varnished until it was now the colour of darkened pine. She balanced her mug on it and stared at the snow in awe. It made her feel like a child again. *In this day and age, this is hard to come by*, she thought, trying hard not to be cynical, but it really did bring out the inner child in her. Oh, how she loved the snow, and as she watched it falling, the memories of her childhood came flooding back.

The first memory of snow she could recall was when she was a toddler. She had tried to clamber up on granny's knee, pointing at the display cabinet where the snow globe sat. She remembered she could not speak; she could just point her finger. Granny knew what she meant, and she would cuddle her into her ample bosom and say, "I know what you want, pet. You want my snow globe."

Granny would put the globe into Bryony's small hands. First, she would look at the globe filled with water. Then she would laugh with granny while shaking it upside down and all around.

Almost magically, it would turn into a tiny world of people going to church with a steeple and snowflakes thick, fast and furious.

Another precious memory began to replay in her head. It was Christmas Eve, and her dad had lifted her in his arms to look outside the living room window to watch the snow falling. As she gazed in amazement at it, Dad whispered softly, "Has the cat got your tongue, pet? It's not often you're quiet for so long."

Bryony stuck out her tongue just to make sure a cat hadn't actually got her tongue. Dad had laughed at her gesture.

"I want to play in it," Bryony had commanded.

"Later. Now I have to get you ready for midnight mass. You're getting a big girl, so this year we've decided to take you to mass rather than leave you with your Auntie Annie."

"I can dress myself," Bryony said stoutly.

"Know, pet, but we are in a hurry. You know Mam; she never likes being late for church. We don't want to be in her bad books, do we?" Bryony shook her head frantically. As much as she loved Mam, she had learnt even at her young age that Mam had a quick temper.

Dad had dressed her in thick black tights, a brown fur hat and a thick brown coat. She even remembered that it flared out at the waist. *I must have looked like a stuck-up wee madam,* she laughed to herself. Finally, Dad had put her two hands into bright yellow mittens dangling from a length of wool that he had placed inside her coat.

After much screaming on her Mam's part at her two older brothers, Liam and Dan, they began to make their way through the woods towards the church roughly half a mile away. Mam and Dad walked slowly, each holding one of her hands. Bryony remembered the clusters of stars in the sky and the sound of feet crunching in the snow.

When she heard her brothers shouting, she looked behind her in alarm because they fought a lot and it frightened her. Mam and Dad were forever giving them rows for it and asking them to stop it because half the time, they were just teasing Bryony. Now they were flinging at each other what looked like hard pieces of snow, loudly laughing as Liam lobbed a perfect snowball straight into Dan's face. "I want to play," she pouted, looking beseechingly at Dad. She knew who she could wrap around her little finger.

"No, pet, you will get hurt," her Mam said firmly.

"Och let her play, May. The laddies will look after her."

Liam then ran towards them and shouted, "C'mon, Bryony, I'll show you how to make a snowball, and then you run and hit Dad with it as hard as you can."

Bryony nodded eagerly; her face was a picture of mischief. "Now let's get these mitts off you," Liam said before showing her how to make a snowball. Bryony remembered running as fast as her chubby legs could carry her and hitting Dad on the back of his knee with the snowball. Much to Bryony's glee, Dad howled with mock pain and shouted, rubbing the back of his knee, "You really have got a good aim, pet." Bryony's childish laughter echoed through the woods. Mam bent down, put her mitts back on and shouted, "C'mon, boys, we have to really hurry now. There will be enough time for playing with the snow tomorrow."

By the time they entered the church, Bryony had started whimpering, which soon turned into full-blown sobs. "My hands hurt, Mam," she cried. "I know, wee lamb, but they will soon warm up." Her Mam's words soothed her as she rubbed her warm hands onto Bryony's freezing ones.

The mass seemed to go on forever. Bryony wished she had stayed with her Auntie now. Her eyes were drooping; she was so tired. After that, all she remembered was Dad lifting her in his arms and carrying her home, whispering that Santa Clause was coming tonight.

Bryony returned to Earth with a start. Her daydream was

abruptly interrupted as her eighteen-year-old son Lee walked into the kitchen, his short blond hair tousled, his feet bare. *God*, thought Bryony enviously; the young ones never seemed to feel the cold, or, maybe more to the point, they could be freezing walking about in a biting wind with T-shirts and jeans hanging past their backsides but would never admit it. Lee poured himself a bowl of cereal and milk and flung himself on a stool at the oblong grey table in the centre of the kitchen. "Did you have a good time with your mates last night?" she asked with an air of innocence. Lee grunted a reply, "Aye, Mam, we were supposed to be just having a few pints and a game of pool." He then held up his hand. "Before you say anything else, yes, I'm suffering, and yes, I was Jim Beaming, and before you ask what those two words mean, yes, I had too much to drink, so I'm hangover. And I don't need any Mother Teresa lectures from you."

Bryony decided to ignore his last remark. Like most people with a hangover, his sunny disposition didn't shine through. *Not that it shone through very much lately*, Bryony thought ruefully. Och, well, her Mam said all teenagers go through that horrible stage, and she wouldn't let him spoil the magical moments of the snow, which was now falling thick and heavy.

"I've been watching the snow falling," she sailed cheerfully. "I just remembered," Lee gasped and groaned, holding his head as he looked through the glass. "I've got rugby practice this afternoon."

"Not if the snow keeps up, you've not. Oh, look, Lee! Look at the wee robin perched on top of the garage."

"I'm not interested in the stupid robin," he said irritably.

"I think it's a miracle really that every snowflake is

different," Bryony replied dreamily. Lee looked at her like she was an idiot.

Aye, it's due to fractal mathematics, nothing miraculous or romantic about it," he exclaimed.

Bryony said tersely, "Look, laddie, you're doing my head in, so just leave me be. Snow reminds me of my childhood, and I don't appreciate any smart remarks from the likes of you."

Lee smirked, "Aye, right. It's a wonder you can still remember your childhood, 'cause let's face it, Mam, you're getting on a bit now." Bryony looked at him, and Lee could see that her temper was rising. *Enough is enough*, he thought to himself. He would be the one who would suffer in the long run. "You just remember, young man, if I'm not happy, nobody in this house will be happy."

"Sorry, Mam," he muttered.

"Look," Bryony said, her face downcast. "The snow has stopped, the sun is coming out and you'll be able to get to the rugby after all."

"Any chance of a lift?" He was using his little boy voice. Bryony laughed out loud.

"No. No chance of a lift."

Lee gave her a grin and, with a quick peck on her cheek, said, "Well, it was worth a try, wasn't it? So you go back to daydreaming about your childhood and the snow, and I'll go and have a shower. You might like watching it, Mam, but I know one thing. For some reason, I will do anything to avoid going out in it," and with that last remark, Bryony heard him pounding up the stairs laughing.

We Are Going Camping But For How Long?

Sue looked up from her ironing as her two sons, Tom, twenty-six, and Aidan, twenty-two, lumbered into the kitchen. "How was your day, boys?" She knew full well it would be the usual tales of woe.

"It was guff, Mam," Aidan said as he casually stuffed crisps into his mouth. "I was giving out advertising balloons outside the optician's shop all day, and this bloke I used to work within the factory passed by and said, 'How's it going, mate?' and I said, 'Aye. I'm living the dream.' I must have met everyone I've ever known standing like a complete eejit, and then to top it all, Gran and her pal passed and decided they would help me give out the balloons. You have no idea of how mortified I was!"

Tom was practically bent double laughing. "What was the slogan on the T-shirt you had to wear?"

Aidan said huffily, "Have a perfect day. Guaranteed when you come into this optician's to have a free eye and hearing test."

By this time, Tom was laughing so much that tears were running down his face, and Sue was the same. Aidan gave him a quick punch on the shoulder and shouted, "If you don't stop laughing right now, I'll punch you where it really hurts."

In a diplomatic spirit, Tom changed the subject. "You know what scares the hell out of me? When I've finished my shift at the pub, sometimes in the early hours of the morning, and I'm walking home, no one is about, and I've got to walk past that cemetery," he said with a shudder.

Aidan retorted, "Och, don't be a daft man. Like Mam's always telling you, it's not the dead you've to be frightened of. It's the living."

"Aye, I know that. Until I have to walk past it on my own."

"You know your trouble; you watch too many horror films," Aidan laughed.

"Oh, all right. I've had enough of you and your psychological mumbo jumbo," Tom said, shaking his head sadly.

Sue looked at them suspiciously. Most of the time, they were in a foul mood when coming home from work. It was the exception to the rule that they were so cheerful. *That pair are up to something,* she thought and knew from experience she would be the last to know.

"Guess what, Mam? Myself, Tom and our pal Ian, we are off on a three-day camping trip from tomorrow," he said excitedly. "We have been planning it for days. It will be an adventure. Camping, climbing in the west of Scotland and fishing too."

"You two have never been fishing in your life, and knowing you two, you will spend it legless in a tent or a pub."

Sue was cross with their plan.

Both boys chose to ignore that remark. Tom said, "We have to go, Mam. Our bus into the city is in twenty minutes, and we have provisions to buy." By now, Sue was even more suspicious.

She watched them striding along the street to the bus stop, blonde hair slicked up. *My God,* she thought fondly, looking at them. It must cost those two a fortune on hair gel, never mind the designer jeans and trainers.

Still, they were good laddies – always looking out for each other. Woe betided anyone who ever hurt the other one. Tom had a devil-may-care attitude, and if he had a hard time, he would simply shrug his shoulders and get on with it, but Aidan was a worrier. *Always had been,* Sue thought. Even if he didn't have anything to worry about, he would find something.

Three hours later, they were back. Sue heard them before seeing them, shouting in loud voices, laughing and joking. *They have been to the pub,* she thought, *but you're only young once – let them enjoy themselves.* She wasn't thinking that a minute later when they stumbled through the door weighed down by the amount of equipment they had purchased.

What Tom had bought wasn't too bad. They had shared the money for the tent between them, but by God, Aidan had really gone to town. He pulled all his camping equipment out of his bags – climbing boots, jacket, woollen hat, socks and sleeping bag (which was beyond her comprehension, as there were two perfectly good sleeping bags in the attic). He knew that fine well. But when she saw the two walking poles, she looked at him incredulously. "For the love of God, Aidan, you told me you were skint. You're going up the west coast of Scotland for three days, not going on a climbing expedition to Mount Everest!"

"I know, Mam, but I've got to be ready for any eventuality," he explained.

The morning they left, Sue took photographs of them as they stood sternly with all their equipment, looking as if they were going off to fight a war. Tom had to help Aidan put on his rucksack. It was heavy, and even though she knew the walking poles should be shortened, Aidan didn't have a clue.

As they were leaving, Tom gave her a cuddle and said, "Mam, knowing Aidan, those useless poles will last twenty minutes. They will be put in the first litter bin we come across. He's already moaning about them."

The following night, she got a phone call from Tom. "Hi, Mam, we have booked ourselves into bed and breakfast, although I have to share a room with that eejit brother. Aidan was useless at assembling the tent, then a gale began, and the tent blew away, and anyway, it was freezing, and by the way, Mam, I was right about those poles going into the first bin we came across!"

Sue laughed quietly to herself. She knew them so well. Three days' camping – not a chance!

Lily's Friends

Lily practically danced along the pavement, her long orange hair swinging to and fro. A woman who happened to be passing by smiled, thinking to herself, *that is one happy lass, though heaven knows what she has done to her hair... by God the colour – it almost blinded me.* To be honest, Lily wasn't too sure about the colour either. Truth be told, people had been looking at her strangely. She preferred her hair colour as it originally was, a soft auburn, but her new friends Sylvia and Dot told her the new colour would give her a glow and much more confidence. After all, as they were quick to point out, who better to rely on for expert advice?

Inside Dot's chic, state-of-the-art home, Lily removed her shoes, elicited a quick hello and made her way to the bathroom. But before entering, she heard Dot drawl in a bored voice, "You know, I can't stand pretending to be Lily's so-called friend anymore."

"Yes," Sylvia's voice rose, "I know exactly what you mean. It started off as a bit of a laugh, but it has become a bit tedious. I'm beginning to detest the ground she walks on – she is so pathetic!"

Lily froze, then mentally willed her body to get to the front door. She had begun to shake, her heart was thundering and with trembling hands, she quickly lifted her shoes. A voice in her head told her to put on her shoes first, but the other voice was screaming for her to just run. Her hands were trembling so badly now that she had to will them into coordinating between themselves into opening the front door. Once she got it opened, she crept into the street.

Her eyes were filled with tears threatening to spill out. Her throat felt raw as she tried to swallow. Unable to breathe properly, she heard with utmost clarity Dot's voice ringing out through the open door. "She's such an old-fashioned dumpy thing hardly in our league. I just took pity on her, really."

Sylvia replied in a clipped, brisk tone, "Oh, I was a tad bored, but now I just find her irritating, constantly looking for reassurance about her appearance."

Dot laughed again. "Wasn't that hilarious – talking her into spending her entire month's wages in a designer boutique and picking out the most hideous clothes for her and us congratulating her on how wonderful she looked… then taking her to the pub wearing those clothes and the felt hat with all those long green feathers that she had to keep removing from her drink!" The two of them, by now mimicking Lily's voice, were laughing hysterically at each other's antics.

Outside in the street, the tears fell silently as Lily chanted, "Just breathe slowly and deeply. You will soon be at Aileen's, and she will help you." She cringed, thinking of the secrets she had told them. Unbelievable now, but they had been so sympathetic. How much they must have enjoyed spreading it all about the village. Among all the overriding emotions, she felt the first glimmer of embarrassment and thought it might overtake other emotions in time, but not just now.

Lily made her way to Aileen's and thumped loudly on the front door. Aileen, Lily's twin sister, instantly knew something was wrong. Nobody created that amount of noise for nothing, and after taking a quick peek through the peephole, she flung the door open in alarm and ushered Lily into the living room.

She finally got the full story out of Lily after a few huge gulps of wine. "How desperate was I for their company? If one of them had told me to jump off the Forth Road Bridge, I would probably have done it. I'm a pathetic excuse for a human being."

Aileen had been so glad that Lily had seemed to have found a niche in the village. She had always been protective of her sister. She had been especially happy that she had become friends with two women in the village. However, she recalled that Eve, her old school friend, had heard whisperings through the grapevine that Lily should watch her step with those two new friends. Aileen had dismissed it at the time. She now realised guiltily she was probably so busy in her own life that she hadn't given it much thought.

As she cuddled Lily protectively, she made a promise to herself. Her way of thinking was not so much turning the other cheek as an eye for an eye, and by God, those two witches from hell would pay for this. They would regret they had ever entered Lily's life by the time she was finished with them.

After Lily had finished telling her story, Aileen's tone of voice was soft and quiet, but Lily could almost feel the anger pulsating from Aileen's whole body. Her knuckles were as white as her face, and her brown eyes, normally soft velvet, were full of menace. Her hand shook ever so slightly as she picked up her wine glass and said in a chilling voice, "It's okay, Sis, by the time I am finished with that pair, they won't be able to lift their evil heads in this village again. But let me give you a piece of advice. Some evil people in this world get their kicks out of hurting those they consider vulnerable, and by God, you are not the first and certainly won't be the last victim. They are in such a sad place themselves that they have to resort to bullying tactics in order to gain power over others and make themselves feel good. But believe me, it's the last time they will ever mess with you. Is it Eve's pub these two witches frequent?"

Lily didn't argue with Aileen, who told her in no uncertain terms that she was staying with her for a while, and once Lily was asleep, Aileen put her plan into action. Aileen was a popular and well-liked figure in the village, and with the help of a few friends, she was going to make those two pay. Whilst the villagers had their share of arguments, most were of the same frame of mind where injustice was concerned. Aileen knew this. The bullying took many forms, and in Aileen's eyes, Lily had been emotionally bullied tonight, and she didn't know how much time it would take to eradicate the hurt – if ever. Hell was too good for the likes of them, and she knew her friends would agree.

A few miles away from Aileen, Eve had her evening all planned. She would put on her old dressing-gown, open a bottle of her favourite wine along with a box of chocolate éclairs and watch an old film. Tonight was a night to spoil herself. She had it all planned. She got much satisfaction and normally thoroughly enjoyed owning the village pub, but she was just too tired tonight. Just as she was settling down to enjoy her evening, the telephone rang. She decided to ignore it, but the ringing was insistent, and, uttering a few unmentionable oaths, she realised there was no way whoever it was going to relent. Sounding thoroughly aggrieved, she barked her name down the phone, and then her face broke into a grin – seconds before it disappeared. By the time Aileen finished reciting Lily's story, Eve had already decided what to do.

"Give me until tomorrow night, and I will come up with something that those bullies never forget," Eve promised. They spoke for a few minutes, and Eve began pacing the living room floor when the call ended.

By the following night, Eve and Aileen had their plan firmly worked out. The hardest part had been confirming to Lily that her two so-called friends had indeed been spreading rumours in the village about her and much worse.

Two evenings later, the plan was coming together. Friday night at the local village pub was always popular. It was karaoke night. Eve knew the "friends" would turn up in their latest designer gear, full of their own importance and no doubt singing into that karaoke machine as usual like a pair of demented banshees. She had a few friends also in the plan, tasked to ply them with drinks to ensure they didn't leave early. Her trump card was her niece Sally. She was young, reactive, sophisticated and stylish. She epitomised what the two "friends" aspired to be, although they would never accomplish it if they spent their entire lives trying.

Sally gave Eve a wink as she slowly and gracefully walked

into the pub stopping at the door for a minute purely for effect. Watching her, Eve thought, *God, she should have been an actress; she will have them eating out of her hand before she sits down.* Sally glided over to the "friends", then both standing at the bar, and introduced herself. Aileen and Eve watched in amusement as Sally showered them with compliments on their appearance. "God, they're practically salivating over her, Aileen."

As arranged, microphones had been placed in the toilets, and as Sally had shown Sylvia new ways to apply the makeup, she asked innocently why their other friend wasn't with them tonight.

"What friend?" they asked simultaneously, and Sally proceeded to describe her. They went into peals of laughter, explaining exactly what they thought of Lily and the gossip they had been inventing about her. They laughed hysterically until they realised there wasn't any music emanating from the pub – just deafening silence. Sally then pointed to the loudspeakers and scathingly said, "You bitches have been caught out, haven't you?"

Fear and horror showed in their faces as they began muttering that it was just a big joke. Lily walked with her head held high. She spoke in a shaky but determined voice as she told them exactly what she and the villagers thought of them, her index finger pointing at them. "Shame on you. There is an old saying, 'As you sow shall you reap', and I hope you both will suffer for the way you made me suffer." With that, she walked away, and Aileen whispered menacingly, "Always remember watch your backs whenever you are in the village. I may not have finished with you yet."

Later, reminiscing over the night's events, Lily said she couldn't believe how the villagers had applauded her. It had all turned out so well. She was laughing as she remembered how those two had scurried out of the pub like mice. She turned to Aileen and asked, her gaze worried, "You were only trying to frighten them, weren't you?"

"Of course, I was," Aileen replied cheerfully as she gave Eve a knowing look, and Eve nodded back ever so slightly.

Artist's Dreams

Aideen sat at the top of a small hill amongst a carpet of bluebells, looking in wonder at the scenery. To the left was a tiny wood from which she could hear a small stream softly gurgling. To her right was a field of sunflowers, their heads dancing gently in the soft breeze. She looked across the turquoise sea to France just several miles away and decided she would have to explore this beautiful place when the sun wasn't so hot. In the distance, Aideen could see the mountains – today, they were a misty blue. She was never tired of how the seasons and the sun changed the colour and the shadows which flowed across them. Sometimes they were almost black, then emerald green, Aideen's favourite colour. It reminded her of her Mam, who was Irish, "and very proud of it too", she had always told Aideen. That is why she was called Aideen. "An Irish name if there ever was one", her Mam would say solemnly like she was reading something prosaic from the Bible. When Aideen was a child, her Mam would sit her on her knee and tell stories from her childhood, Irish folklore and legends.

She never got tired of the stories her Mam would weave,

whether truthful, imaginary or perhaps a mix of both. She smiled at those memories. A soothing breeze blew gently through her short brown hair, a welcome relief from the heat of the blazing sun. She was so glad she had moved here from Glasgow. Not that she didn't love Glasgow, but it always seemed to be raining, and she loved the warmth here. She had at first been apprehensive about uprooting herself and all she had known, but it had seemed like a gift from heaven when a post for a primary school teacher on this island had turned up. Although she missed her Mam dreadfully, it was Mam who had said firmly in her usual no-nonsense attitude, "Aideen, don't throw away what God has offered you. Grab it with both hands, and besides, I can come for a wee holiday now and then. Just imagine I'll find an excuse now to buy myself a whole new wardrobe of summer clothes instead of Arran sweaters and wellies."

Aideen had managed to get herself a tiny flat, and she loved her job. Most of the children were a pleasure to work with. She smiled again as she remembered teaching children on the beach yesterday – that would never happen in Glasgow. With her outgoing, friendly personality, she quickly made friends with the locals.

She saw some of her new friends in the distance, a group of artists at their easels painting and drawing. Apart from a few bees buzzing around and the sound of waves lapping gently onto the shore, there was silence. They were so engrossed in their work. They were of various ages. Trevor, the youngest of the group, looked like he should still be at school, but then she thought, that's what happens as you grow older. Everyone starts to look so young. Sometimes she still felt like she was eighteen until she looked in the mirror. She laughed aloud at that thought. Ron, hearing her laughing, turned around to wave, and Aideen waved back vigorously. He called himself an ageing hippy and was so much fun – he just didn't take life seriously at all. He maintained that everyone had to have a dream, and painting was his. He then would convulse into fits of laughter. Aideen was never sure whether he was taking the mickey out of her. She smiled again as she remembered Ron telling her a five-year-old could paint better than she could, and she had joked back that he must be the oldest hippy she had ever had the good fortune to meet. All said with warmth and laughter. Annette was in her late sixties and had taken up painting when her husband died. At first, painting was a form of escapism, but it quickly became her solace in getting through her darkest days. It gave her a purpose in life. Todd was the shy and serious one of the group and had stated that he was painting to try and pay off his debt by selling his work. Then there was Aviva, who constantly waved her heavily jewelled hands in the air and who said she had more money than God. Still, she found it hard to make true friends. Her friends, she had discovered, were usually more interested in her money than in her, but in this little group, she had met decent and kind people who didn't care about her money. She was now in her eighties, and her attitude was that she had spent her whole life being a people pleaser, running after others and never making herself happy, but she was happy now.

Aideen so envied them; imagine being so engrossed in your work you could forget about your worries and cares for a little while. She looked out to the shimmering sea and the cloudless blue sky and knew from their finished work how each one viewed the scene before them differently. It was true; people could look at the same view and paint a different picture from their perspective. She knew better than to disturb them but also knew they would be delighted to welcome her once their painting session had ended. Soon it would be lunchtime. That's when she would go and join them and sit outside the pretty little village pub, which was adorned with colourful hanging baskets and tiny fairy lights woven through the fence.

They also sold cheap and delicious food, which would be accompanied by a few bottles of local homemade wine. Aideen loved listening to their banter, different views of life, problems and happiness. They sold their work to the various craft shops in the small town and were unfailingly polite to the tourists who walked up to stop and look at their work. After all, as Todd stated, they were the people who gave him a livelihood.

She looked at her watch, it was almost lunchtime, and they all began to make their way to the pub. Aideen so loved this time of day; they were all such fun. As she walked down the path, she thought that no matter her personal worries and fears, she could cope with anything with this little group of artist friends beside her.

Eavesdropping

Nina sat comfortably in her old multi-coloured deckchair at the top of her tiny garden, straw hat covering her snow-white hair, sunglasses on to keep out the glare of the hot sun. *Well*, she ruefully thought, *it certainly isn't going to prevent the wrinkles, that's for sure.* Now, well into her seventies, she was well past worrying about her appearance, not that she had ever worried about it in her younger days. She had always been amazed when many of her admirers had said she was a beautiful woman. She took a sip from her favourite drink, gin and tonic, and laid it gently back down on the tiny wooden table by her side. She could feel herself drifting off into a light sleep.

As she dozed, she remembered her younger days. Back then, she had never been concerned with her beautiful looks, just amazed that it seemed important to her admirers and drew the envy of other women. Perhaps it was also her outgoing personality and her lack of airs and graces that drew men towards her like a magnet. But the love of her life was anthropology and reading, much to the dismay of the men she met up with.

She had had a few serious relationships and even moved in with one man, Eric. Once she had moved in with him, it lasted less than six months. He was possessive and smothered her. He had reminded her of a puppy, constantly trying to mollycoddle to please her. At the end of six months, she knew she couldn't wait to get away from him. He was irritating her; plus, she loved her independence. He wanted to accompany her everywhere she went, so she left before she really began to despise him. She knew she was a horrible cow to him at the time but couldn't help it. When she finally told him it was over, he was heartbroken, but she heard through friends that he had married a few years later. She had been happy for him.

She had never had another really serious relationship or gotten married, and she had never had any desire to have children. So when acquaintances asked if she was thinking of settling down and having kids, she would vehemently dismiss their questions with a firm "Never." They would raise eyebrows at each other and look at her in astonishment.

She had a happy life, good health, many friends and her beloved anthropology research. Also, thousands of books were crammed into every nook and cranny of her home. She finished her dozing and took another sip of her drink, thinking she was truly satisfied with her life – even more than that, she was content.

She was startled out of her daydreaming when she heard her next-door neighbour's back door slammed shut. Her neighbour was Laura, who had two sons, Sam, aged nineteen, and Jon, eighteen. She heard the boys making their way into the garden shouting at each other like they needed hearing aids. They flung themselves onto sun loungers, and she could hear the sound of beer can rings being pulled. "This is the life," she heard Jon say.

She smiled. They could both be wee imps but, at heart, were good laddies. Anytime she needed help, they were always there, obliging and never making her feel like she was bothering them. Similar in looks – tall, slim, blonde and blue eyes – a stranger would easily spot them for brothers, but that was where the similarity ended. Sam was bossy, and although they could fight like cat and dog, she knew they were very close to each other. Sam was always reprimanding Jon, and Jon would often tell him fiercely to shut the hell up. However, Laura had told her he listened to the advice Sam gave him more than he listened to Laura – "Well, most of the time," she would say disapprovingly.

"These shorts are coming off," she heard Jon announce. "Aye. I think we need an all-over tan. Why not? There's no one to see us except old Nina, and she's always asleep at this time of the day." *Wee devils,* Nina thought with a smirk. *I've a good mind to peek my face over the wall and see their reaction. Auld Nina indeed!*

There was silence except for the greedy slurping of beer. Jon, who finished his beer first, said to Sam, "I'm going in to get another beer. Do you want one?"

"Aye," Sam replied and then said lazily, "just bring out the whole crate."

Jon sounded horrified. "Sam, if Mum finds out, she will kill us."

"Listen, stop being such a wimp. When we've finished the crate of beer, we'll take it to the dump and get rid of it. Mum won't be home for hours. If she doesn't see the empty crate, she'll forget we had beers in the house."

Nina put her hand up to her mouth just in case they heard her laughing softly. *By God*, she thought to herself, *Sam swears like a trooper*. He can't get a single sentence out of his mouth without an F word. If Laura heard him, he'd get a good clip around the ear and another clip around the other ear for both of them drinking their way through a crate of beer.

Jon spoke next, his voice slightly slurred. "Know what, Sam? I hate being on the dole."

Sam gave out a groan. "Not this again. As Mum would say, you're like a broken-down gramophone record. God, will you shut your gob about hating being on the dole? That's all you rant on about."

"It's all right for you; you're an engineer," Jon grumbled. "You know what I feel like? I feel like a jaikie with all the rest of those on the dole. We go into that Job Centre, and I feel like a stray dog, a loser, treated with contempt, and I know I'm much more intelligent than they give me credit for."

Nina heard Sam give out a huge sigh, and as he answered Jon back, she detected a note of impatience in his voice. "Listen, mate, the reality is that you're unemployed – I know you don't want to be, but the fact is that you are. It's not your fault, and you're not a jaikie. You can't be that much of an eejit. For your work placement, you were picked to go and actually work in the Job Centre, and the staff was really kind to you. They took time off without hesitation for appointments, bringing you sandwiches they had made up along with their lunches at home. They even gave you a huge box of chocolates and a card to say how much they appreciated the effort you had put in working with them. You could easily have been sent picking up litter off the streets instead."

"But I wanted to be sent to work in a museum," Jon said petulantly, sounding to Nina like a six-year-old. By this time, she could hear Sam really starting to lose his temper.

He now shouted at Jon, "You better shut up now because you're really starting to get on my nerves. My one day off work, and I've got to listen to your whining. Millions of people have got it harder than you, but it's all about you, isn't it? If you don't shut your gob, you're in danger of me doing it for you."

Nina knew that Sam would never hurt Jon physically; he would just stomp off and leave Jon to his own devices and feel sorry for himself. "I'll tell you something else. Maybe I do have a paid job, but it isn't exactly a holiday camp either. So c'mon, lighten up; working in the dole office can't have been terrible all of the time. You must have had some laughs with your so-called other jaikie mates that came in to find work."

Sniggering, Jon began, "You're right. So there I was, filing work onto the computer. I have to say, most of the people who came into the office looking for work were really pleasant. Then this guy came in, and when the consultant told him to go on the computer and look for work, in a really gruff voice, he scratched his head and said, smirking, 'I canny work a computer missus, I'm computer illiterate.' 'Computer illiterate, are you? Well, we will get that problem sorted out immediately. I will be sending you on an IT course starting next week.' 'What do you mean?' The guy said in total disbelief and alarm, 'I don't want to do an IT course.'"

Jon was now really laughing out loud, "And then the consultant said, 'You either go on the course or your benefits will be stopped.' He had only said that because he couldn't be bothered working on the computer, and it really backfired on him."

Both of them were laughing now, as was Nina, trying to stuff a hankie into her mouth to silence herself, but it was too late. They had heard her. Both looked over the fence, shocked that she had been listening to their conversation.

"Did you hear all of what we were talking about?" Jon asked, his speech slurred.

Then, in her thick Scottish brogue style, Nina decided to brazen it out. "I did, young man, and I suggest, Jon, you get away to bed before your Mam gets home. Do you think she's completely daft? You both smell like a brewery. Sam, you take those Carlsberg cans to the rubbish tip and get Jon away to bed."

She then said sternly, "I didn't realise you had a mouth like a gutter, but don't worry, my lips are sealed," as she made an imaginary zip-seal across her lips. "I think both of you are going to be in enough trouble when she sees the state of young Jon here."

If Laura finds out I know about this afternoon, I'll be in even more trouble than those two put together because I haven't told her, she thought to herself.

"Sorry, Nina." They both looked totally contrite.

"Well, get cracking then. I've got more worthwhile jobs to do than lecture you two."

They both hurried away as Nina watched them. Well, Sam walked away. Jon staggered. Once Nina was in the safety of her kitchen, she laughed until tears rolled down her cheeks. *Eavesdropping beats daydreaming any day*, she thought.

Dreams of Italy

As Cathy hung out her washing on the line, she wondered why she bothered. Maybe it was her upbringing. Her Mam's hands had been blue and swollen, but she always stuck to her laundry regime. If it wasn't raining or snowing, the washing had to be put out on the washing line. Maybe subconsciously, she had picked up the obsession from her.

She looked up to the leaden sky and watched a formation of hundreds of geese making their way south for the winter. She didn't know much about the formation of geese flying above, but she knew the oldest flew first. *It must be heaven*, she thought wistfully, *to move to warmer climates in the winter*. She watched them fly until they were tiny specks in the sky.

Never mind. Today the boring housework could wait. After all, she would have to do it all again tomorrow. She would take out her globe and look at all those countries she had never seen and was never likely to see. She could spend hours looking at her little globe. She supposed it was her hobby, the way other people studied the stars or completed puzzles.

Once the housework was done, just enough for it not to look a total mess, she made herself a mug of tea, took out her globe and spent the next hour letting her imagination run riot.

Italy was her favourite place on the globe, and she was determined to visit there one day. In her mind, she was already in Italy, in a small village twenty or so miles from Naples, standing in the kitchen of her whitewashed villa. She pictured herself dressed in a short yellow cotton dress and silver pumps with sunglasses perched on her head. She had a honey-coloured straw hat and an old-fashioned basket she had found in the tiny hall to carry the groceries she would need to last her a few days. And of course, she had her camera. She vowed she would take hundreds of photographs to take home. It would be even better than looking at Italy through her globe. The kitchen was bright and airy, painted sunshine yellow with terracotta flooring. A pine table stood in the centre of the room with a large wicker basket filled with Sicilian lemons surrounded by a large midnight blue pottery jug full of garden flowers. Gleaming copper pans hung on the walls, as did bunches of onions, herbs and garlic. Tea light candles adorned the villa; she thought the person who owned this beautiful place must be really into candles. The one-bedroom was welcoming and cool, but it was the kitchen she loved the most.

She instinctively knew why she loved this room. It had a floor-to-ceiling window with spectacular views of distant snow-capped mountains that reached the sky. She could see how the sun danced across them and cast shadows that fleetingly changed the colours. Across the villa was a small deserted white sandy beach, with the waves lapping onto the shore. Cathy thought the lapping sound of the aquamarine blue waves was soothing, gentle. The small garden was an array of flowers, including Cathy's favourite – sunflowers. Two pear trees stood on either side of an oversized hammock strategically hung to catch the sun. The olive trees in the garden swayed ever so lightly in the soft, warm wind.

With her imaginary sunglasses on to protect her from the glare of the sun, she began walking around her imaginary village. Life seemed so laid back, with the narrow, cobbled streets and the faint noises of Italian music coming from the local tavern. The air was scented from the hundreds of vividly coloured flower baskets lining the streets. Old men sat outside a cafe smoking their pipes, laughing and joking with each other, and although Cathy could understand little of what they said, they were obviously having a good time. Small boys played hide and seek, running up and down the streets. Old women sat on steps dressed mainly in black, embroidering lace handkerchiefs, talking nineteen to the dozen. With arms around each other, young lovers slowly strolled around the cobbled streets. For a few fleeting moments, she wished she had someone to share life with. Cathy gave herself a mental shake. After all, she was an eternal optimist. What her future travels might bring was anybody's guess. She laughed out loud at the thought. The old men and women had seemed posed when Cathy had held up her camera and gestured that she wanted to take photographs of them.

She sat outside a little cafe drinking delicious Italian coffee, noticing how kind the waiters were to the old people and young children.

Her next stop was the local market, and she strolled slowly among the stalls listening to the laughing and bantering of the stall owners. She admired the Italian food for sale – luscious thick minestrone, huge olives, fresh ravioli and crusty bread. Also, there was an assortment of fruits and cheeses and her favourite Italian dessert, Tiramisu, with layers of thick double cream which, they assured her in broken English, was freshly made every morning. She adored the sounds and the smell from the stalls selling Italian flowers. The atmosphere quite simply made her feel alive and happy. She could have wandered around the market and the streets all day just peering into shop windows.

Where else could she go? Perhaps a picnic on the beach so she could sit and gaze at the far-off mountains. Or maybe back to her cottage and straight into her flower-filled garden to lie in her hammock and doze gently, the Mediterranean sun warming her face. Tonight, she would have supper outside and watch the clusters of stars.

There was a loud bang, and Cathy sat up with a start. She had dropped her globe. She smiled to herself and placed it back on the table. She poured herself a tiny glass of wine (Chianti, of course), sat back down and closed her eyes. Italy was nice – maybe Greece next time.

The White Feather

Large fat tears rolled down Sammy's cheeks as she sat huddled on a log in her favourite part of the forest. Shimmering bluebells surrounded her with the morning sunshine filtering through the trees, causing the dew on the grass to glisten like millions of jewels, but Sammy was oblivious to the beauty of it all.

When had it all started to go wrong for her and Ian? she repeatedly asked herself, but in her heart, she knew.

It had started so well. Sammy had gone for a few drinks at a pub near the university campus, and as she looked towards the bar, she saw Ian and was instantly attracted to him. Seemingly, he felt the same way. He smiled over to her, she smiled back, he asked to buy her a drink, and for the rest of the night, they sat together, laughing and joking, discussing university life, its upsides and downsides. Sammy was in her first year studying for a degree in English literature, and Ian was in his last year studying law.

From that night, they became almost inseparable. Sammy felt like she was walking on air; she was so happy. Sometimes she just could not believe this dark-haired, handsome man with the gentlest brown eyes could be in love with her. God, he could have had his pick of a woman much more attractive and outgoing than her. How could he have fallen in love with her?

Before too long, she had moved out of the tiny cramped flat she shared with her best friends Em and Jayne and began living with Ian. When she first saw his flat, she gasped in astonishment at its utter luxury. She had always known Ian's parents were wealthy, but she had no idea they had this kind of wealth. "They pander to my every whim. Not for me the life of a poor student," Ian beamed. Of course, he was joking, but it crossed Sammy's mind for a few seconds that he sounded slightly pompous and smug.

They had been so happy together, Sammy thought. She worked hard getting through lectures and exams. Ian left university and began working for a prestigious law firm and quickly began to climb the professional ladder. With Ian's ambitious streak, Sammy knew he would rise quickly.

After a year of working and playing hard, living and loving together, it all began to change. At first, trivial things caused problems, like Sammy forgetting to put the dishwasher on or forgetting to bring home a carton of milk. Sammy had always known that Ian could act like a petulant child sometimes and treated him accordingly, laughing it off with Ian grinning back, but now he was sulking for two days or so at a time. It had got to the stage that Sammy felt she was walking on eggshells, not knowing if she was coming home to another one of his black moods or the loving, carefree Ian that seemed to be increasingly disappearing.

Sometimes Sammy wondered if Ian was deliberately trying to pick an argument just for the hell of it or as an excuse to storm out of the flat to go drinking with his new posh pals he had met at the law firm. He would come back in the early morning hours, usually having had too much to drink, which would cause him to fly off the handle at her the next morning because he had a hangover.

Sammy seized on any signs he was back to his old self again, and she could pretend their relationship was back to the way it used to be. She made any excuse she could think of for his mood swings.

They didn't go out together anymore. It was usually with Ian's friends when they did, and Sammy hated it. He would drink too much and start making snide jokes about her working-class background and accent. One of Ian's friends would laugh at the jokes, but the others just looked embarrassed and uncomfortable.

Occasionally Sammy would have a girls' night out with Em and Jayne. Once the wine started flowing, Sammy would sometimes let slip some of the hurtful remarks Ian had made to her. Em and Jayne had been scathing about Ian; they both thought him a pompous spoilt ass. As Sammy sat on the log, she cringed with embarrassment when she remembered she had thought her friends were jealous that someone as special as Ian could be so in love with her, when all they were doing was trying to show their concern and being protective of her.

The final straw was one night when they were in a restaurant with the usual group of Ian's friends, and Ian began the by now expected insults. He started off by mocking her working-class background. "It was a wonder she knew which cutlery to use to eat her meal." But then the verbal attacks suddenly became more vicious – attacks on her mom, dad, siblings and friends. Apparently, she was a thick cow and lucky he put up with her. Finally, something in Sammy's mind snapped; she grabbed her jacket, flung his glass of malt whisky over him and fled the restaurant.

Luckily, she managed to quickly hail a passing taxi before the tears began to flow. The concerned taxi driver asked her if she was okay. The journey seemed to take forever; by the time she reached Em and Jayne's front door, she was sobbing uncontrollably. They took one look at her, their faces full of concern, and immediately ushered her into the kitchen, where Em filled a huge glass of wine and thrust it into Sammy's hand. Sammy held it with both hands. She was shaking helplessly, but after a few gulps, the sobs were in control, just tears now as she told them the state of her relationship and especially the way Ian had treated her tonight, the horrible things he had said to her.

By the time Sammy finished her stories, both women were furious. Jayne clenched her fist and shouted, "I'd like to go and punch that arrogant bastard's lights out," and then, with a sudden gleam in her eyes, she shouted, "I know. I'll get John to do it." John was a boxing fanatic and in the boxing ring every chance he got.

Sammy somehow overcame the tiredness and said in a small voice, "No. As much as I'd like to see him suffer, I'll find another way."

Her two friends sat up with her until the small hours, not talking, just listening. Although they knew he had been treating her badly sometimes, they were worried that physical violence would follow if it hadn't already started. They knew in snippets of Sammy's conversations that Ian didn't like the clothes she wore, her hair, makeup, lifestyle and especially not Em and Jayne. She had become a shadow of her former self, with little confidence in her ability to live the life she wanted and practically no self-esteem.

The next morning after a few hours' sleep, Jayne collected John's van, and the three arrived at Ian's flat to collect Sammy's belongings. Sammy insisted on going into the flat herself and assured them that if she needed help, she would holler, and they would hear her okay. When Sammy quietly told Ian she was leaving before he crippled her psychologically and would never return, he looked at her incredulously. Then, he went almost apoplectic with fury. He banged his fist on the table, shouting that no woman had ever left him before. He was the one who ended relationships, not the other way around. Sammy knew then he had stopped loving her a long time ago. Ian showed no remorse at her leaving, only deep anger. Sammy walked slowly away and didn't look back.

As she dried her eyes on her jacket sleeves, she took large gulps of air. God, she was lonely and so scared of the future, and that was when Sammy saw it – the most exquisite white feather drifting gently from the sky until it lay a few yards from her feet. When she was a child and fretted about school or failing the class tests, her Mum would cuddle her close and comfort her, saying that in times of worry and sadness, sometimes an angel in the shape of a feather came near her to let her know she was not alone.

Sammy picked up the feather and gently stroked it before laying it down on the grass again, thinking there was always someone else out there in need of help. She watched her two friends walk through the forest and sit on each side of her on the log. Em squeezed her hand and said, "God help the next eejit who gets in tow with him. Come on, Sammy, we are going out for a night on the town to get plastered. Let's go home to get all glammed up."

Then with a laugh, she said, "You never know; it just might be my lucky night."

Jayne laughed back. "Aye, in your dreams, pal." In spite of the tears, Sammy started to chuckle.

"You remember, Jayne, when you wanted John to punch his lights out, I remembered a quote from the poet George Herbert." At this, the two friends let out mocking groans knowing how Sammy could bore them stiff with her English literature references. Then Sammy said softly, "Living well is the best revenge," and unusually for her friends, they didn't make fun of her. Instead, they slowly began to head home to get all glammed up for a great girls' night out.

The Northern Lights

Katya sat in her garden on an old rickety chair dressed in bright red pyjamas. She contentedly sipped a mug of coffee and lifted her elfin-shaped face towards the sun, which was already warm. Unusually for Scotland, it had been a glorious Indian summer. She ran her fingers through her short bobbed black hair. Yesterday, she had finally plucked up the courage to get it cut short. It felt so light, and it was strange to feel the soft breeze gently caressing her neck. She actually had a neck! Nevertheless, she was pleased with the transformation – she thought it suited her, and it didn't really matter what anybody else thought.

She looked at her small garden – how she loved it! Completely secluded and a perfect sun trap, it was just big enough for Jon to cultivate his tiny herb garden. He was like a five-year-old, out every morning to see how much they had grown overnight. She would bet on it. He even had a special name for them all. Other than the herb patch, there was enough room for a small table, a few deck chairs, a barbecue and, when weather permitted, a sun lounger on the small patch of grass. An apple blossom tree was in a corner at the bottom of the garden – their wee garden in heaven.

She smiled now as she heard a crash from the kitchen and Jon swearing. He was like a bull in a china shop, she thought fondly.

"You can come in now. The car is all loaded, so all you've got to do is get changed, and we're ready to go," Jon shouted.

Honest to God, she thought, *you would be forgiven for thinking I was half a mile down the road, not four feet behind him.* Katya gave him a mock salute as she made her way into the bedroom to get herself ready, and shortly afterwards, they had left Glasgow behind and were heading north.

Katya smiled up at Jon. It was good to get away from the city for a day. Jon wholeheartedly agreed. He had been secretly worried about her. Every day was an uphill struggle for her, with her dad being so ill and in hospital. There were only the two of them, no other relatives. Jon knew his parents loved Katya and vice versa, but it just wasn't the same, and just lately, she seemed to have one bad cold after the other, not her usual healthy self.

Today, Katya was dressed in an emerald-green knee-length summer dress speckled with tiny gold threads and green ballet pumps – only for effect; she had never done a minute of ballet dancing in her life. With her sunglasses perched on top of her head, she looked happy, full of life and eager for their day out.

Jon smiled and touched her knee as she sang tunelessly to 70s music on the radio. It was the Rod Stewart hit, *Maggie May*. Katya knew the words by heart, and she bellowed them out. *Honest to God,* Jon thought, *she has a voice like a foghorn. She just doesn't know it.* Katya glanced over at him and saw the smile on his lips. "Are you laughing at me, Jon?" Her eyes were suspicious.

"No," Jon lied unconvincingly. "Just remembering the 70s, that's all."

But Katya was now in her little world, drinking in the beauty of the scenery – the rolling hills, the endless fields, trees and rivers, the colour of the sky and so on. She hadn't realised how much she missed this – it was good for the soul.

"Nearly lunchtime," Jon exclaimed. "I'm starving."

They drove into the car park of a small, whitewashed pub. Hanging baskets surrounded the pub, a dazzling display of brightly coloured flowers. Instinctively, they made their way towards the beer garden, which was secluded; they were the only ones there. A small fish pond lay in the centre of the garden. They stood for a few minutes watching the fish swim among the water lilies. Katya picked out the bench in the corner of the beer garden surrounded by trees shading it from the sun. A tiny lit white candle had been placed on the wrought iron table in front of the bench.

After a delicious meal of homemade salmon fish cakes and salad with lots of crusty bread, they finished a bottle of red wine, most of which Katya drank. After that, they joked and laughed and strolled around the quaint little village, wandering along the narrow street, peering into the windows of craft and pottery shops and admiring the baking smells wafting from an old-fashioned tearoom.

It was hot now. They sat down on a tiny wall beside a water fountain. Katya must have dozed off for a few minutes. A combination of the warm afternoon sun, meal and wine had made her tired. She awoke to feel Jon nudging her arm as he handed her a tiny dark-blue box. On opening it, she found a tiny pair of silver earrings in the shape of a half-moon – she had admired them in one of the craft shop windows. Katya gave out a whoop of delight and kissed Jon firmly.

Leaving the village behind and driving further north, they finally stopped in a lay-by. They left the car and saw a small wooden gate. The path led through a tiny wood where bluebells and heather grew in abundance.

"Listen, Jon," Katya whispered, though why she was whispering was beyond Jon's comprehension; there was no one around for miles. "Let's walk a little further. I'm sure I hear the sound of running water." Finally, they came to a clearance between the trees, and Katya clapped her hands in delight.

"Look, Jon, isn't it beautiful!" Katya exclaimed like a small child. They had reached a shallow flowing stream where the water was so clear they could see the shining stones at the bottom. "They look like they have been polished, Jon!"

"They *have* been polished, you eejit, by the time and the water," Jon said as he brushed a strand of hair way from her face.

Katya gave him a withering look and said, "Shut up, Mr Know-it-all." She peered into the flowing water again and shouted, "Jon! I can see tiny fish in there."

She then flung off her sandals, wrinkled her feet in the soft grass and dipped her toes in the water. Although the water was cold, it was refreshing. She lifted handfuls of water to wet her face, arms and legs. The water sprayed around her, casting out what seemed like thousands of diamonds playing in the air as they caught the rays of the hot sun.

Jon took a bottle of white wine from the cool box and poured Katya a glass. As she turned around, momentarily stopping from splashing in the water, she laughed.

"Remember, Jon, the last time we had a day out, you in your wisdom decided to keep the wine bottle cool by surrounding it with pebbles and stones in a stream to keep it cold? The next thing we knew, it had been swept away, and you had to run hell for leather through the water to try and catch it." Katya was laughing out loud at the memory of Jon soaked to the skin and her screaming, "Keep running, you will catch it eventually!"

"Aye, I caught it alright," Jon said wryly, "about half a mile downstream," and then he began to laugh too.

They lay on the blanket, enjoying the silence, broken only by chattering birds and the sound of the stream, the water relentlessly cascading down the hillside.

"C'mon, sleepy head, time to get moving if we want to get to the loch before it gets dark." Jon took her hand to haul her up, and Katya knew instinctively that Jon had missed his favourite loch and now it was so near he was itching to get there.

At last, they were there. The loch was, as ever, unchanged – beautiful and also frightening, Katya remembered from when she was a child. Back then, everything in life seemed so big, but as you became an adult, the world could become surprisingly small. However, to Katya, the loch and the surrounding mountains looked the same – simply huge. Jon stood silently in awe of the majestic mountains. Katya rushed down the tiny, pebbled beach, exclaiming, "Look, the mountains are yet to have snow on them. Over there on the left." In Katya's eyes, the glittering loch, the snowy mountain and the twilight sky seemed to merge into one.

They stood together looking at the loch. So still, so silent. The mountains and clouds were reflected in the water. As they stood staring at the reflection, the sinking sun began to change the reflection on the loch, turning it to a shimmering burnt orange.

As Katya sat on the tiny, cobbled beach, she watched Jon skim pebbles across the water and proudly thought he was quite an expert at this. Her best attempt was getting a pebble to skip twice before disappearing. But she dismissively retorted to Jon, "Well, I can't be good at everything."

It was growing colder now. Katya and Jon knew how chilly it could become and were dressed in thick warm jackets. While Jon began cooking on a small campfire stove, Katya lit outdoor candles.

"I'm starving. Must be all this fresh air," Jon groaned.

Katya's mouth watered as Jon expertly cooked two sirloin steaks marinated in barbecue sauce, husks of corn on the cob and baby potatoes melted in butter with fried tomatoes. Apple pie and cream washed down with their favourite wine quickly followed. Afterwards, they sat watching the stars come out. The sky had now turned to an azure blue.

Jon began, "There is the Polestar, the Great Bear and Vega."

Katya looked at him disapprovingly. "Stop right there Jon. I only want to look at the stars. I don't need a science lesson."

Katya could look at the twinkling stars for hours, whereas Jon had an avid interest in astronomy and would bore her stiff, going on about all the different stars and their names and constellations. She didn't really want to know how stars were actually formed. They had arguments about that before. Sometimes she thought he did it just to wind her up. But, finally, when he started one of his lectures, she said, "I mean it, Jon, you are really doing my head in."

The campfire was just cinders now, only the outside candles burnt, and the stars lit up as darkness descended. They sat in silence for a few minutes, and then Katya whispered to Jon, "I think there is a searchlight, Jon. it's spreading out and covering the whole of the northern sky."

"It's the Aurora Borealis Katya. The Northern Lights."

She looked at him dreamily. "I don't care what the name is. It's so beautiful." Then suddenly, the whole northern sky became a sheet of yellow and green resembling rippling curtains rising from the horizon. Pinkish flickers of light appeared here and there, and they danced like flames across the darkness. Then they would fade and begin again in a different place a few seconds later.

"I have never seen anything so beautiful, Jon," Katya sighed.

As Jon gazed up at the spectacular sky, he simply said, "We may never in our lifetime see anything like this again."

Katya giggled, making violin gestures saying, "Oh, give me a break, will you?"

Katya took his hand in hers and asked quietly, "Do you think you can see the sky in heaven?"

Jon squeezed her tightly. "I'm sure you can – only nobody will be lecturing anyone about where stars really come from and how they are actually made."

Katya. smiled and leant closer to Jon, both of them tiny dots against the horizon.

The School Uniform Shenanigans

Pat and Tony let out sighs of relief at once as they dumped themselves on the living room sofa. Pat impatiently pushed aside her dark curly hair that covered her face and said, giggling, "How is it that we still end up going shopping around this time when we know that the supermarkets are packed with screaming parents and kids frantically trying to get uniforms before school starts after the summer break?"

Tony grinned at her, saying, "Let's not go down that road. Thinking about it still gives me a headache."

Pat smiled at him. To her, he still looked the same old Tony that she had met at a bus station thirty-five years ago when she had been a rebellious teenager. That day, she had asked him cheekily for a light for her cigarette. She knew full well from her friend Cathy that he was a fitness fanatic, so she was fully prepared to hear the usual speech about how smoking is so terrible for one's health. Surprisingly, he just smiled and said, "Sorry, I don't smoke." She had fancied him for ages, and from that day, they fell in love and had never looked back. Tony was heavier, greyer and more lined, but he was still her Tony as she was his Pat; the time had never changed that. Tony asked her with a smile, "Penny for them?" She smiled back. "They are not worth a penny."

Suddenly, their youngest sons Ken and Scott sauntered into the room. Thirty-year-old Ken was a younger version of his dad, tall and fair, whereas Scott looked more like Pat, having blue eyes and a smaller, stockier build. Thankfully, both of them took after their dad in temperament, being quiet and soft-spoken. It took a lot to arouse anger in them, the exception being their favourite football team being beaten), whereas their older brother had a temperament more like Pat's, impatient and fiery. Funnily enough, despite the differences in their character traits, on the whole, they all got along really well.

"What is it that you said about school uniforms, Mam?" Ken asked.

"We were just talking about how nightmarish shopping for school uniforms for you three used to be," Tony replied.

Pat drifted off into her own wee world; memories that had been stored away were now surfacing after she had seen the families today; the fraying tempers, the tears, the screeching tantrums… *God, it had brought it all back.*

Pat remembered herself and Tony snuggled up in their big bed, each trying to cajole the other to get up and tell the three boys it was definitely the day to go and get new school uniforms. No more faking stomach aches or feeling sick. All the excuses under the sun had been tried. They both dreaded it, knowing the crying and pleading would start and then the tears. One son was bad enough, but three? They felt like their heads were ready to explode.

After receiving the great news that they were indeed going

shopping for school uniforms, in stony silence, the boys gave their parents "the look," which they had down to a perfect art, and flung themselves into the back of the car. Wearily, Pat asked if any of them needed to go to the bathroom before they left, which was again met with stony silence. Then, they were off to buy school uniforms and all the paraphernalia that went with them.

The car journey always seemed endless due to the boys' bickering. A sneaky nip was given and given back, usually with the younger two coming off the worst. Threatening them with the usual *no television, no sweets and no football* was like water off a duck's back. They were too busy squabbling, and any warnings were simply ignored – they knew their parents inside out. As usual, it was Pat who cracked, ending up screaming at them. It annoyed her, even more, to see that not only the boys but also Tony was laughing at her. By the time they got out of the car, they were all practically best pals, except for Pat who was now in a furious mood and ignored the rest.

Pat remembered her sons being in primary school when she could cajole them into wearing cheaper school shoes as long as they were allowed to pick out their own rucksacks. But as they began secondary school, it really did become a nightmare. She recollected how tight-lipped Tony would become, obviously considering the finances in his head, as the boys demanded their own special brand of what they deemed school wear and all the trappings to go with it. More often than not, the boys would have to settle for something not at the top of their list. Both Pat and Tony remembered thanking God that the school the boys attended had a strict dress code, so in the end, they mostly had to abide by the school rules.

She couldn't even begin to imagine the nightmares other parents went through for those children who went to schools where students could wear whatever they wanted as long as it was, in the schools' eyes, "decent."

As Pat was talking about it, the boys began remembering it too. Pat and Tony looked at each other and smiled as both the boys said at once, "Do you remember that?"

"Aye, that sick feeling in my stomach when Mum and Dad would wake us up to tell us we were going shopping," shouted Ken.

"Yeah, they would already be in a bad mood before they would wake us up." Scott said and continued, "It was those stupid signs in the shops, 'Back to School'. Oh, how I hated them. Were they trying to make us miserable? Also that smell in the shoe shops, I'll never forget that smell, leather and shoe polish. Now, I really am starting to feel sick, no kidding mum."

Pat started to laugh.

Now, Ken piped up, "Remember that really nasty shoe-shop assistant who looked as old as the hills, forcing my feet into those horrible black shoes and me looking around for Mum who was too busy arguing with Lewis? Lewis was insisting that he wouldn't be seen dead in the shoes Mum had picked out because the shoes were 'guff' and he would look like a 'right geek'."

Both the boys were now in fits of laughter, but Pat wasn't finding the memories too funny now, thinking had she had really not noticed that shop assistant being nasty to Ken. Scott made the situation even worse by saying, "Mind Mum, those big blisters I had on my heels because you wouldn't listen when I told you the shoes hurt my toes, but you insisted that horrible shop assistant had fitted my feet correctly?"

Tony noticed the hurt on Pat's face and said in a strict no-nonsense tone, "If I were you, I'd stop taking the mickey out of your mum."

Pat was indeed starting to look quite upset, so Scott said apologetically, "You know we're only joking, Mum; just winding you up."

Pat looked at them, wondering if that had really happened because she honestly couldn't remember it, but by now, they had moved on to another tale of woe. "Remember mum and dad used to say schooldays are the best days of one's life. I wonder what bright spark made that one up," Scott said. "Scarred me for life it did, going to get those uniforms and then having to face a year of school."

"Och, give it a rest," Pat retorted. "You two you don't know how well-off you were. Go on, Tony, you tell them about what our grannies and granddads put up with going to school."

It was said half-jokingly, but when Tony had taken an interest in genealogy and found out about their great grandparents, they were both shocked and saddened by the hard lives people had back then. When they all sat together looking at Tony's family history archive, the couple was surprised to see how much interest the boys had shown in learning about the older generations, whom, up until now, they had known practically nothing about.

Tony said, "My dad never spoke too much of the hardships in the 1920s and 30s and the hunger and poverty suffered by his parents and thousands like them, but all he ever did say was, 'There were no good old days'."

Silence fell as each of them thought about the remark, and then to lift the gloom that was descending, Pat said, "Och, to hell with the time. Let's all have a wee dram."

Pat and Tony smiled at each other as Ken and Scott began arguing over who got the biggest dram. Tony playfully cuffed Scott's head, "When you were kids, we had to make sure that you all got treated the same with your school stuff. You were never happy and always complained one had been favoured over the others. Tonight, it's an argument over who has the biggest dram. Some things will just never change around here."

Intangible

Within my earliest memories, I occasionally felt a fleeting presence with me – a gentle whisper of a delicate breeze softly caressing my cheek, sometimes a tiny far away laugh. It was nothing remotely scary; in fact, it used to make me giggle because, in my mind, I was playing a game with myself. I often got tired of the game because, like most children, I had the gift of living in the present moment and was more concerned with what I would buy with my threepence, a weekly gift that came from my gran when she collected her old-age pension, than I was about any ephemeral presence.

On this beautiful September morning, the last thought on my mind was about my childhood. It was a day for fully living in the present moment, and after a horrendous bout of flu, I was away from the dingy, dirty claustrophobia-inducing city where I lived.

So determined was I not to miss a single moment of my day that, for a change, I was packed and ready to go early in the morning, pleased with myself that I had my mobile phone, a bottle of water, a quick snack and of course, sun lotion. One of the disadvantages of being a redhead is that I burn within two minutes of walking in the sunlight. I tied back my long hair quickly, placed my sunglasses on the top of my head and set off, reminding myself to get as many photographs as possible to show Jan. Jan was my friend who, incidentally, was still in bed with the flu. As I strolled through the soft grass, meadows and woods on either side of me, what hit me almost instantaneously was the pleasant air. God, I took in a huge breath; it smelt so clean and fresh and unlike anything I was used to. Then I took in the view, focusing first on the bushes of wildflowers including bluebells and the trees enveloping me. I feasted my eyes to the distant yet breathtaking snow-capped mountains, so majestic they almost took my breath away. The rising sun gave my world a soft peach-coloured glow, and as I watched the sun first peeping and then rising from behind the mountains, I shouted, "This is the life," not caring if my voice was carried into the distance.

The sun was warm, so even the weather was on my side, and as I rambled along through the soft grass, my mind felt lighter with each step. The problems of my life in the city then seemed to melt away. Finally, in a clearing through the woods, I noticed a bright blue wooden poster, dangling from a rope tied between two trees. Looking at the sign, I smiled. It said, "The Old Barn Cafe" in what was obviously a child's handwriting. I could not help but imagine a child's little face deep in concentration, attempting to write the words.

The cafe, although empty, was exactly as its name stated – an old barn with benches, table and chairs out in the sun. There was even a hammock with a few children's toys strewn around it. A smile came to my face, and I could just see in my mind's eye an exhausted parent lying there, having a well-earned rest with one eye on the child playing. The furniture was made of wood, and the tables and chairs were covered in emerald-green checked tablecloths. In the centre of each table was a small glass milk bottle, spilling wildflowers that were obviously picked from the meadows. Again, with a grin, I said to myself, "A child's hand at work here." Besides the small tables, there was a huge table, running the entire length of the barn. My imagination was running away with me now; I could just see my friends and I spending a couple of days here, walking and having a real shindig here at night. Fairy lights and candle lanterns were hung up all around the barn, and as I walked behind the barn, a field with tables, chairs and barbecues came into view. Everything for enjoying a summer's evening was there. Attached to the left side of the barn was a tiny indoor shop, selling home-made wines, beers, chutneys and jams. I vowed that on my way home I would buy a few jars of gooseberry and ginger jam. Gran used to make it for me before arthritis made it impossible for her to do so, and seeing the jars of jam conjured up all the old memories of me sitting in her kitchen, devouring scones and jam.

    I wandered through an orchard full of apple trees and strawberry plants and then sat down on a wooden bench directly opposite the barn entrance. With my eyes closed, I sighed deeply, letting the sunlight warm my body and dance on my face. I felt utterly content and could feel myself gently dozing off, and then I recalled the memory from my childhood. Now I felt the presence, a soft caress on my cheek, the same tiny laugh as if to say, "All at peace in your world." I didn't want to let go of this feeling, this intangible presence, but I slowly opened my eyes and returned reluctantly to the real world.

And then I saw her. A girl was sitting on a bench directly opposite to me, about sixty yards away. She was in her twenties, thin and tanned; she had short black hair, and she was smiling gently across at me. I smiled back. Instinctively, I knew that she also knew about that intangible presence, or perhaps she was that intangible presence, or maybe to her, I was that intangible presence. There was no communication between us except for that smile. I knew I would never meet her again, but I also knew when I had felt that presence that it could be from her and perhaps the intangible presence she had felt could be from me.

As I walked on, a realisation slowly came to me: there are both shadows and rainbows in everyone's lives, and when the shadows come, I wouldn't feel so lonely and hopefully neither would she, due to that intangible presence we shared at that moment.

Enchanted Woods

Melissa stood at the entrance of what she liked to think was her enchanted woods, which seemed to go on forever in her eyes. The early morning mist had disappeared, and the sun's rays were golden yellow, lighting up the dew like thousands of sparkling tiny diamonds. Melissa thought *I could stay here all day.* With her long, black uncombed hair and her pink wellingtons and yellow jacket, a passerby wouldn't have missed her, but she was lost in her own thoughts. Her friends would have laughed if they could now see Melissa, who is usually a chatterbox and the life and soul of any party; her large brown eyes were now staring silently transfixed at the rays of sun dancing through the trees and illuminating the bluebells.

The woods were silent except for the chirping of birds, and Melissa heartily welcomed the solace. All her friends, including her long-time partner Alan, considered her a city woman. She was born and bred in Edinburgh where she still lived. She totally loved city life, the hustle and bustle, crowds, noise, the trams and buses and the chaos of it all. Alan thrived on city life too.

But sometimes in an almost subconscious corner of her

mind, there would flicker a desire to become one with the natural world that she had long forgotten. She chuckled at the thought of this, but the woods gave her a sense of peace she could not get from restaurants, pubs or friends. She found her soul here, and her friends would be bewildered by this affinity of hers. "Melisa walking in the woods with a pair of old wellingtons on and a fleece?" They were more used to seeing her at shopping malls or parties. The parties she threw were renowned, and anyone who has been to one of them was forever asking when she would be having another one.

The woods gave her time for contemplation. As she gazed around, she took in the beauty. She never felt afraid here; she revelled in the solitude. She listened to the gurgling of water and watched a tumbling brook carry water that sparkled in the rays of the sun. She looked at the silver birch trees and laughed to herself. The woods had so many different varieties of trees, but the silver birch trees were the only ones she could recognise. But what she definitely did recognise was the sweet smell of the bluebells, which grew in abundance, and in the sunlight, they looked white and dazzling. She basked in the morning sun, and she lifted her hand to push her hair away from her face, her silver bangle glistered in the light. She raised her smiling face towards the sun. She then removed a blanket and a tiny flask of coffee from her rucksack and sat down. First, she looked at the clear blue sky and then at the greenness of the trees and the beautiful sunrays, glinting through the canopy.

The mass of bluebell flowers seemed a thick blue carpet, and Melisa felt like taking her wellies and socks off and wading through them, feeling their softness and the dew on her feet.

Melisa heard footsteps and whistling and knew at once it was Alan, her boyfriend, coming to look for her. She knew him so well that she didn't even have to turn her head to see who was approaching. He smiled down at her, gave her a quick kiss on her cheek and said, "I knew I would find you here," as he handed her a bacon roll. They then sat together in silence for a while.

After some time, Alan broke the silence, "It's lovely here, but we have so much to do today. We have a party to organise for tonight and shopping to do, not to mention the cooking."

Melissa sighed softly as she began putting her blanket back in the rucksack. She said, "Yes, I suppose so," and got up to leave. As they walked out of the woods, she held Alan's hand and said earnestly, "You know, Alan, I sometimes think I could be one of those eccentric people living in the woods in a caravan. I'd be as poor as a church mouse, but I think I would be so content and happy."

Alan looked at her incredulously and suddenly burst into peals of laughter, which reverberated through the stillness. "Melissa, you wouldn't last a week here. Not without your designer clothes and fancy wine bars."

Melissa frowned and looked at him despondently, and she felt her eyes moistening.

She let go of his hand and turned away before the tears started, suddenly realising that he didn't actually know her at all.

In fact, nobody did.

The Young Un's Perspective

Beth, dressed in old jeans and a pink sweatshirt, carelessly tied back her blond shoulder-length hair into a ponytail and caught a glance of herself in the bathroom mirror. The special-effect LED lights her boys had installed in the bathroom should be banned, she thought. Okay, if you were twenty years old, you could just about get away with it, but today, she just groaned loudly. She looked pale and gaunt, there were dark circles underneath her brown eyes, and her roots definitely needed to be redone. It would take a beauty expert to make her shine, that was for sure, but she was recovering from a bad bout of cold, and to be honest, she couldn't have cared less about her looks.

All in all, it had been a horrible week. Mr Gibbons was her employer, whom she worked for as a cleaner at his mausoleum of a mansion just outside the village. *Cleaner?* she thought to herself. *Dogsbody maybe? Let's face it,* she thought to herself furiously. *A servant from the Victorian era would be more like it.* He had been particularly nasty towards her this week, and she had felt so low within that she didn't have the energy to respond to him as she normally would do.

He was such a rude man. Sometimes Beth wondered what had happened in his life that could make him that cruel to people; how many excuses could you accept? He truly believed that he was still lord of the manor, strutting about the village, barking orders to whoever happened to cross his path. Beth shook her head despondently. Poor old Mrs Brown who still worked in the local post office and was eighty actually shook like a leaf when he entered her shop. She would never forget that day when he had caught Tam, his gardener, eating an apple that had been picked from his orchard. Beth had thought he was surely going to clobber Tam with his walking stick; his face had turned purple with rage, and he was screaming like a banshee.

It was an utter waste, thought Beth crossly. The boughs of the trees bent so low with plums and apples. Three greenhouses were filled with tomatoes, cherries, peppers and chilies; another one housed exotic flowers. Rather than give them away or sell them cheaply to the local market stalls, he just let them rot.

At best, he was the most obnoxious man she had ever had the misfortune of meeting let alone work for, and at the worst, he was the devil incarnate. Why, just last week Beth had been finishing off sweeping the kitchen floor, leaving the house immaculate, when there was a heavy knock at the door. She heard Wayne, her oldest son, quietly asking if his mother was ready to leave for home, explaining that it was snowing heavily and there were no street lights until they reached the village. She heard Mr Gibbons bellowing to Wayne that he had no business to be looking for his mother as she hadn't finished her chores yet. Wayne had stood his ground and repeated in a low-pitched but firm voice that he was there to give his mum some company on her walk home.

She couldn't help but smile when she heard the door being slammed shut and Mr Gibbons making his way into the damp, dingy library, but not before banging his walking stick on the walls as he proceeded. She donned her warm coat, wellingtons and gloves and shouted in the direction of the closed library door that she would be in to work next week. Outside, Wayne was stamping his boots furiously into the snow. Beth was unsure if it was in anger at the way he had been spoken to or due to the freezing temperatures or perhaps a mixture of both. Beth smiled at him as he switched on the torch. Taking his arm, they began to slowly walk home. The wind was picking up now, and Beth muttered to Wayne how cold it was. Wayne clearly wasn't interested in the weather.

"Mum, you have always stuck up for yourself, so why do you let him bully you? If Jack had been here instead of me, he would have punched that old man's lights out, and it's not the first time I've heard him treat you like you're a piece of dirt."

Beth knew full well that what Wayne was saying was true. *If my sons knew the half of it*, she thought.

"I've heard the villagers talking amongst themselves at the pub, Mum, about the fact that he's a nasty piece of work and the abuse they have to contend with when he has to pay their wages for working on his farm. He still thinks he's the lord of the manor."

"Yes, I know. Let's change the subject now," Beth said with a sigh, "We don't want to get Jack on his high horse. He can rant and rave the night away if he feels inclined to."

Wayne laughed out loud. They both knew exactly what

Jack was like. When he set his mind on something, he was like a dog with a bone.

Beth made her way into the kitchen, shouting at the boys who had started bickering over some stupid computer game. She could feel tears stinging the back of her eyes as she looked at the mess. Unwashed breakfast dishes littered the boards, and there was an empty packet of cornflakes, the remnants of which had been scattered on the kitchen table, as well as a pint of milk, she swivelled around and stared dismally at piles of dirty laundry. Was it just her or why did they need handfuls of bath towels for one bath?

They were still bickering – *Honest to God*, she thought wearily. It was hard to believe Wayne was twenty-one and Jack eighteen; between listening to them and looking at the mess, you would have been forgiven for thinking she had two four-year-olds at home. No, that wasn't true. Two four-year-olds were no doubt better behaved. They must be the untidiest creatures God had ever put on the face of this planet. She couldn't even be bothered shouting at them again.

Beth made herself a mug of tea, sat despondently at the kitchen table and stared out of the window. It was snowing heavily now; huge fat snowflakes whipped against the window, and with one hand resting on her chin, she watched the boys plonk themselves down opposite her. *Their natures are so different*, she thought as she appraised them, and yet, they could almost be taken for twins. They were both tall and lean, although how that came about was beyond her comprehension - it seemed that every time she looked at them, they were eating. The difference between them was their eye colour; Jack had piercing blue eyes that seemed to have a constant mischievous twinkle. As Beth looked at him, she knew full well who was the brains behind all the childhood pranks. Wayne's eyes were the colour of dark chocolate – he would break a few hearts in his lifetime. Wayne had managed to get a full-time job at a computer firm, and Jack was trying to get some part-time work near his university. He was home for the Christmas holidays and already driving her insane, constantly complaining that he was bored.

Wayne muttered an apology about the mess made in the kitchen, kicking Jack underneath the table, telling him to apologise too. Beth looked at the two of them and said in a flat, weary voice, "I've had it with you two. You know how hard I work at that old mausoleum of a house up the road. Just clean up after yourselves."

"It's a dishwasher; we need Mum," Jack piped up.

"Any more of your smart comments and I think I'll hit you one myself," Wayne said scathingly, and Jack gave out another yelp on receiving another kick from Wayne.

"What are you thinking, Mum?" Wayne asked, looking at her directly; he was more sensitive of the two of them.

Beth sighed, her hands clasped around the mug of tea, and said dreamily, "Do you really believe that millions of people actually live like that?"

"Like what, Mum?" Jack asked, puzzled, thinking his mum did waffle sometimes.

"You know, on a Sunday morning, lying in bed with real percolated coffee, not the instant stuff we drink, reading a book or a newspaper, then having a leisurely shower in a perfectly gleaming bathroom and having another coffee in a warm fluffy bathrobe, then getting dressed casually in a warm jumper and jeans, depending on the weather, sitting out in their conservatory or on the patio, sipping a glass of champagne and then walking to some old world pub, having a sumptuous bar lunch and cracking open a couple of bottles of wine with friends; and then going for a walk through the woods or a park to come home to an immaculately decorated and spotlessly clean house."

At this last remark, she shot both of them a filthy look.

"Och, no Mum, most folks live like us, just plodding along," Jack smirked.

"Well, not according to the books I read," Beth said crossly.

"Aye Mum, but the books you read are rubbish," Jack admonished. "That time you had the flu, I was fairly embarrassed to go to the library to get you that stuff."

Wayne whispered to him, "Don't push your luck; we are on our last legs with Mum, and you know what she's like when she loses her temper. All hell breaks loose – so how about shutting your gob?"

"We have a wee surprise for you, Mum," Jack said, grinning from ear to ear.

"Oh, yes, and what would this surprise be?" Beth asked suspiciously. She had had plenty of wee surprises as they were growing up. Her grumpiness was now disappearing; they weren't bad laddies, just hard work.

Jack began, "Well, we know you've been a total crab lately," and then faltered as Wayne gave him a warning look. "No, I take that back, Mum. We have noticed you've been a bit down with dad working away and having to work for the devil himself. So, Wayne and I are taking you out for a bar lunch today, and we will do all that rubbish those yuppie folk do in your books, and we are paying," Jack said proudly. Then amended it with, "Well, Wayne's paying."

Beth clapped her hands in delight and then ran upstairs to get changed. Wayne grinned at Jack and said, "That was a good idea, mate; shame I'm paying for it."

"I'll give you my share when my student loan comes through," Jack promised.

"I know you will, mate. C'mon, let's give her a treat."

And what a great time was they all had. Beth dressed in what she called her "decent clothes," sat at the kitchen table with a glass of – no, not champagne, even the lads couldn't go that far – white wine and then dressed for the snow. They walked a half mile to the old pub. They sat beside a crackling fire, drinks in hand. Beth appreciated the fact that the pub had no huge televisions, with the sound blaring out so that you could hardly hear what anyone was saying. There was just some quiet music in the background. A large Christmas tree stood in a corner, covered in silver and red bows. Jack was acting like a child as every so often, he would sneakily take one of the chocolate decorations from the tree and pop it into his mouth. Beth felt happy and as warm as buttered toast as they laughed and joked with each other. For starters, it was pea and ham soup, then homemade steak pie, chips and peas for Jack and Beth and scampi, chips and peas for Wayne, washed down with a bottle of red wine.

On the way home, no walk through the woods or park; even Beth admitted it was too cold. With her arms tucked through Wayne's and Jack's, Beth laughed and said it was a wonderful treat. Jack laughed back and said, "When we get home, Mum, you put your feet up, and Wayne will fix you a wee brandy, and while you're at it, Wayne, you can make it a double for me, and remember, it's my turn to play the computer game."

"No, it's not," Wayne shouted. Beth smiled, telling them both to shut up. Well, they had been wee angels for roughly two hours, and she was beginning to wonder how much longer it would last.

When they reached home, Jack lit the fire, and the lamps gave a warm glow. Although the house was immaculately clean, it was maybe getting slightly shabby, Beth thought, but if Owen did get this promotion at the car plant, life would start to look up and she would be able to give up her horrible job and go to college to begin what she had always wanted to do, jewellery-making.

Jewellery-making, she thought, as she sipped her brandy. She might just make some money out of that wee venture. Well, you never know what surprises life might fling at you. Look at how badly this week had started and how well the evening had turned out. Life is like that.

Hide-and-Seek

A passer-by who wasn't paying much attention would only have seen two little girls running through the woods, hands tightly entwined. The elder one had long blond hair streaming in the wind, and the other had shorter shoulder-length brown hair and was perhaps a few years younger.

But if the passer-by had looked more closely, they would have seen the fear and panic in those little faces as they ran.

Zara ran blindly through the dark forest, her hands sticky with lollipop sherbet firmly holding her little sister Molly's hand. Her heart was pounding. She felt like a big man's boot was stamping on it over and over. Her sobs were becoming hoarser and faster, and she could taste the blood in her mouth from her bitten tongue. She kept on repeating to Molly like a mantra, "Run faster, Molly; just keep running, don't look back." Molly was whimpering as Zara urged her to go faster. "C'mon Molly," she pleaded, "I've got a secret hiding place that only Josh knows about; we'll be safe there. We'll be safe from that bad Harry, and when Dad finds out he frightened us, he will give him a good leathering, you just wait and see." She caught a glimpse of Molly's tear-stricken face; her bright blue eyes full of terror, her dark hair matted and dirty and her forehead bleeding with a gash caused by a passing branch. Zara mustered all the courage she could.

"I'm a great big girl who's nearly eight, and she's only five, so it's up to me to keep her safe." She was so frightened. Thoughts, silly thoughts, kept coming to her mind about how mad Mam would be when she finds out her pinafore dress was torn, and then the horrendous overriding thought that Harry would hurt her and Molly, especially Molly.

She really hated Harry. Mam said one should not hate anybody, but she really hated him. Sometimes she had caught him looking at Molly in a way that made her feel uneasy, in a way she couldn't completely understand. Something within her told her it wasn't a nice feeling and that she should mention it to Josh or her mam and dad, but she never did. Oh, how she wished she had told Josh now. Maybe he would have listened and not told her to shut up because Mam had always said to him, "Now, you look out for your two wee sisters, young man," and usually he did unless they were really annoying him, but he would never have let Harry hurt them.

Their pace was slower now, and Zara winced as her hair caught on a sharp branch. While pulling her hair free, she thought she heard footsteps crackling on the dry bracken, so without turning around, she began running with Molly again. The forest was becoming denser now, and up ahead, she could see a small hill covered in green fern. They ran to the back of the hill where Zara pulled apart a large clump of fern and climbed into a small crevice-like hole; there was just enough room for herself and Molly. With all the strength she could muster, she pulled Molly inside and tried to reassemble the fern and bracken to its previous state.

The hole was dark, cold and damp, although a tiny chink of sunlight managed to get through the clumps of fern above. When they had both got their breath back, Zara put her index finger to her lips so that Molly knew not to make any noise. They sat together, clutching each other, for what seemed to Zara like hours, but in reality, it was only a few minutes. Inside, they could hear just the silence. No birds chirping and more importantly, no footsteps.

Zara began to whisper to Molly now and cuddled her in close. She couldn't see Molly's face but could taste the mingling of blood and tears. Zara held her even closer and even managed to give herself a half-smile when Molly whispered she was holding her so tight she couldn't breathe. Zara strained her ears for the slightest noise outside, but all she could hear was the pounding of her own heart as well as the soft breathing of Molly who had fallen asleep.

As time passed, the chink of light seemed to get duller, and Zara thought it might soon be night-time. Her thoughts were all jumbled now. She was scared. Maybe, Mam and Dad would never find them. Josh knew about this place. Suddenly, she was swept over by a terrible panic, *What if he had shown Harry the secret hideaway?* She pushed away that thought instantly. She would never be able to stay in control if she had terrible thoughts like that, and although Mum and Dad hadn't come for them, neither had Harry, so that must mean he didn't know about this secret place.

Zara and Molly had never liked that horrible Harry and didn't know why their brother hung about with him. He was fourteen, three years older than Josh, and he was always ordering Josh about and being a big bully. She remembered that time he had kicked Josh really hard and he had screamed out in pain because Josh wouldn't steal beer and whisky from old Mr McKenzie's grocery shop. When she did tell Josh that she didn't like him, Josh told her not to be so stupid. But she reasoned, *If she were so stupid, why didn't Josh want Harry to meet Mum and Dad?*

Harry had always seemed to want to play hide-and-seek with them, and until today, it had been herself, Molly and Josh together who would play at finding Harry and vice versa, but today, she couldn't find Josh at their usual meeting place, only Harry. When she had asked Harry where Josh was, he said he was away on an errand for his dad. Zara thought that was a lie. Dad was working away from home, so how could he have sent Josh on an errand? But dad often said there were these things called white lies, and they weren't really lies. When she asked Dad what he had meant, he had begun talking about something else, and she'd forgotten to ask him again, so maybe Harry's lie was a white lie and that was alright.

When Harry suggested playing hide-and-seek, Molly began jumping up and down, yelling how much she loved the game. But Zara didn't like the way Harry was looking at Molly. He kept on staring at her and roared he was the big bad monster and that he would find her. He began to laugh. It was not a funny laugh, and Zara decided she didn't want to play this game. Molly must have sensed her sister's fear because she was no longer yelling in excitement. She was hiding behind Zara's pinafore dress, sucking her thumb, a gesture from babyhood that returned when she was nervous.

Harry had now turned his back to them. His face was against the tree trunk and his voice was muffled, but Zara heard him say, "I'm counting to one hundred, and then I'm coming after you both, and it will be Molly first because she's my favourite. I'm coming after you, Zara. I'm coming after you, Molly." That's when fear took over, and they began to run.

Molly was now awake and fretful. Zara found some of her dad's pan drops in her pocket. They were sticky, but they both sucked hungrily on them.

Molly whispered, "Mam and Dad will be grass-hopping mad 'cause I've lost my green ribbon."

Zara whispered, "Don't you worry about that. Tell you what, why don't we think our prayers instead of saying them out loud as we do with Dad every night."

Molly whispered, "Will God still hear them?"

"Of course, he will," Zara whispered back. She wondered whether she was telling a white lie. She would have to remember and ask Dad about that. Then, they both solemnly squeezed their eyes shut.

They both fell asleep, but after some time, Zara wakened with a start, remembering where they were. It was very dark and cold now, and she knew it was night-time. She was shivering and began rubbing Molly's arms trying to warm them, whispering that they were safe and it was all going to be all right until Molly's frightened whimpering stopped. Zara slowly moved her stiff legs and, trying not to panic, realised that she was going to have to come up with a plan.

Finally, she decided that no one good or bad was coming into the cave for them. It seemed Josh had forgotten all about his hideout. *What a thicko*, she thought furiously. Quietly, she explained to Molly they would have to leave the cave and try and find their way home and that no matter what happened, she was never to let go of Zara's hand. She was to do exactly what Zara told her to do and remember that the dark was their friend and no one could see them. She reasoned that if they stayed in the cave, they would just become colder and colder. Zara thought she was trying to convince herself as much as she was trying to convince Molly, but Molly seemed quite content with the explanation, and together they got up to leave the cave.

The stars were shining, and for that, Zara was grateful. The same woods they had played in now looked so menacing; nevertheless, she had to try and find her way home in the dark. Together, they made their way down the small hill and began to walk through the woods, Zara's senses finely attuned to every noise. Her eyes were becoming accustomed to the darkness, and she could see the tall black trees more clearly now. Molly's cold little hand clung to hers trustingly.

As they walked, Molly thought that she had always been terrified of that horrible Harry. Sometimes she had dreams of him snatching her away from her family. Sometimes he touched her legs; once he had squeezed her leg so bad she had a bruise on it, but she had told her mam she had fallen off her skateboard. She was too scared to tell her mam the truth in case he came after her, and now, almost all of her bad dreams about him were coming true. She gave out a little moan, and Zara whispered to her to be quiet.

They kept on walking, but Molly was getting worn out. She had wet herself but was so tired she didn't care. Zara urged her to keep walking because if they didn't, she said she might not wake up – she had heard about people falling asleep in the cold and dark and not waking up.

Zara suddenly felt so exhausted that she just simply fell on her knees not caring if she and Molly would die, which was when Molly shouted, "Look, Zara, I see a light not far away." Zara slowly lifted herself up. A light could be seen through the space between the trees. It wasn't moving, so it couldn't be a torchlight, meaning it wasn't Harry. They both stood still for a few seconds and then Zara said urgently, "I think it's a house, but be deadly quiet in case it's not," and Molly took in the unspoken meaning. They treaded ever so softly now, tired, weak and no longer able to weave away the branches grazing them, and finally, they ended up outside a small old wooden house that had light beaming out of its kitchen window.

The figure in the window let out a scream, and then an old man and woman could be seen coming down the four wooden stairs towards them. Zara began to cry to her own tears, sounding like a wounded animal, whereas Molly stared straight ahead, silent and immobile. The old man picked Molly up in his arms gently, and the woman put her arms around Zara. Slowly, they made their way into the house.

Much later, it seemed to Zara they were in a hospital room, but instead of noise and bright lights, the lights around her were dimmed and didn't hurt her eyes so much. Both herself and Molly had their legs and arms bandaged, and there was a huge swelling on Molly's head. Dad was speaking softly to a doctor. At least she thought that's what she was because he had a plastic thing around her neck like Dr Jones at the surgery. Dad bent down and said soothingly that they looked like they had been in the war but that they would be fine in a few days.

Zara remembered serious-looking people speaking to her and Molly about Harry. Two women said they were special police who would look after them and talk to them whenever they wanted. She and Molly trusted them. They were always smiling and telling them little stories that made them laugh out loud.

Their dad told them that Harry had been caught by the police and they never had to worry about him again. Even Josh had hugged her and said he was scared of Harry too and was glad the police had caught him. Mam and Dad had gone crazy at him and were giving him a life of hell and a whole new list of chores had been drawn up for him besides the ones he already had. Josh looked at her in that embarrassed way he sometimes had, saying, "Dad says I'm a lucky laddie that he didn't skin me alive and that I should go hang my head in shame for getting in tow with the likes of Harry."

For being so grown-up and brave, she was given her first-ever mobile phone, and Molly was gifted a brand-new wooden swing that Josh had painted in her favourite colour, a glaring pink. "Come on, Josh, I want you to push me on the swing," she said. *Quite the little madam,* Josh thought grumpily, and with a look of utter boredom, he agreed. Happily, they ran to play in the garden; Molly's bad dreams of Harry had disappeared, and he was becoming a distant ever-fading memory in her mind.

A Scottish Miners' Gala from a Child's Perspective

Catching glimpses of the sun shining through a chink in the curtains, Jessica snuggled even deeper into her warm duvet – reluctant as yet to face the outside world. This was unusual for her as she was a "morning person," but after slowly recovering from a bad bout of flu, she pretended to herself that she needed pampering.

Today was the local children's gala day. Many from the mining communities were either dead or had moved away. It wasn't like the "old times," the auld buddies in the village lamented, where generations of the same family came together to laugh, reminiscence and play, but the gala day was still important in the community.

Jessica's thoughts slipped back in time to the gala day of her childhood. She was born at the beginning of the 1950s, and the excitement of that day still had Jessica smiling.

She remembered that it had seemed to take hours before her mam was satisfied that her children looked their best, although she must have known full well that five minutes into the gala, all four of them (Jessica and her three brothers) would look like they had been pulled through a hedge backwards. The second they got into the park, every parent made sure that the rarely used camera would be put to good use before their children were set free.

The villagers stood outside their front doors with their banners, flags and gala hats on, waving and cheering to the music of a pipe band as the parade passed by slowly. But Jessica wasn't interested in any of these; all she looked for in the passing crowd was her dad.

"My dad's in the gala committee, you know," she said haughtily.

"Fine, I know. You've talked about nothing else for days," her friend Mary said snarkily.

Jessica chose to ignore her and thought she was a jealous bitch just 'cause her dad spends all his wages and knocks her mam about whenever the fancy takes him. It was the talk of the village. The grown-ups thought children didn't know, but they knew more than they ever let on.

Mam shouted at her and her brothers, "Come inside the house so I can make sure you're all well turned out." They all let out a groan but did as they were told. As Mam looked over each one of them and for what seemed to Jessica like the umpteenth time, she gave a nod of satisfaction. "Well, you lot are as good as you'll ever look."

In a fleeting moment, Jessica remembered pulling at her Mam's dress and saying, "You look nice too, mam."

Mam had tried hard that day; all of the villagers did. She had on her one-and-only special dress, lipstick and perfume that she used for rare occasions like when she and Jim attended the local church new year party. Excitedly, Jessica lined up to walk in the parade behind all the important people. Everyone gave a loud cheer as they began marching, waving their flags frantically and stamping their feet.

They inched their way towards the park beside the primary school. Deck chairs were hoisted out for the auld yins, and the park soon became a sea of tartan rugs on which everyone flung themselves down. The children were usually first to fling themselves down unceremoniously but were given short shrift by their mothers, "Here, get your backside off the rug this instant; it's for Mrs Nelson down the road."

Even before they could plan their escape route, they were given their orders. The older sisters were to take turns to look after their wee siblings, and as for the boys, their job was to continually make their way back and forth to the tea urn to collect the endless mugs of tea for the women. Jessica gave her cousin May a smug look. She had no brothers or sisters and therefore, to her way of thinking, no one to look after.

"And you can wipe that look off your face," her granny shouted, "You're to help your cousin May."

Jessica began going into a temper tantrum before Gran said sternly, "Any more of that young madam and you won't be getting your tuppence this Tuesday when I get my pension." Jessica, realising she was fighting a losing battle, gave in and she and May began walking the toddlers through the park, hoping they would soon fall asleep if they lay them down on the grass.

Jessica and May had a great time at the gala, mimicking the Scottish country dancers. Soon it was time for the men in their kilts to fling a huge log, to which the girls yawned in boredom, but their excitement increased as the races were about to start. It was a foregone conclusion as to who would win the races, the same boy and girl every year it seemed. Everyone knew they would be coming out of the winners' tent with their shilling and a "silver" trophy, and everyone had to applaud and look thrilled for them even though the boy was a bully and the girl a bitchy cow – in Jessica and May's opinion anyway.

The girls had a hoot at the egg-and-spoon and sack race even though neither were in the least competitive. They just wanted a good laugh at each other, and neither was disappointed when they went sprawling.

"It will soon be time for the bags," May said gleefully while licking her lips. "Now mind, Jess, me and you have made a pact. Whatever one doesn't like in their bag, we exchange it with one another and no one else."

"Okay May, don't get your knickers in a twist," Jessica laughed as May stuck out her tongue, making a face at her. "You know fine well that every year we get the same in our gala bag, and I always take the caramel log, so you have my empire biscuit."

At that point, May's stomach rumbled, and she said longingly, "I wish they would hurry up and ring the stupid bells. It's time for us to queue up for our bags."

"Come on, we'll stand in the queue anyway. Look," she said pointing a grubby finger, "the queues have already started." Off they skipped, discussing what they would buy at the ice cream van with their sixpences. Finally, they got their goodies and their mouths full of scotch pie. Jessica still swears the gala pies were the best pies she had ever eaten.

They sprawled themselves on the grass, having swapped

the cake and chocolate with each other and with their Irn-Bru bottle nearly empty and the drink dribbled over their faces and down their necks.

"Now, for the best part," Jessica said and without saying another word, they raced off to the ice cream van, clutching their sixpence in their sweaty hands like they were pieces of gold. Looking back, Jessica thought that ice cream man must have had the patience of a saint to put up with the ear-piercing noise of squabbling kids who couldn't make up their minds what to buy.

And that was the end of the gala day, helping the mums with the younger ones who were fractious and not used to the noise, carrying home the heavy bags with all the paraphernalia in them and at the same time wondering where all the men had gone that afternoon. After setting up tables and doing "men's work," the men seemed to have vanished. Anyone passing the local pub knew exactly where they had escaped to, as the noise of a jukebox blared out and the air was full of the smell (or stench in Jessica's view) of beer. At the door was a cluster of women threatening that if the men weren't home at a reasonable hour, there would be all hell to play when they did come home.

Jessica, unlike May, didn't have to worry about her dad; he liked to keep on Mam's good side. A little later, she raced down the road to meet him; he always had a wee present for them, the same present he always got – a pink pony drink for Mam and a Milkybar for the kids.

It had been a great day, Jessica thought sleepily as she snuggled into her bed covers, and Mam, usually so meticulous, even let them go to bed without a wash!

Mischievous Angel

Every so often, God lets her leave heaven, just for a day, knowing full well she will cause trouble all along the way.

With her bright red hair flowing and her face alight with glee, she shouts, "Angels, look at me. I'm off to do God's work, so you lot behave yourselves, and don't be worrying about the likes of me."

She roams around on her tricycle, though secretly wishing it was a bicycle, her chubby little legs pedalling furiously, enjoying every second of her day.

With her fierce shout, "Hey you lot, get out of my way. I'm here to do God's work, and I've only got today."

She cycles down the motorway and through the supermarket too, helping herself to goodies to gift to her chosen few.

The villagers all gaze in amazement as jelly babies fall from the sky as she shouts, "Oh, what a kind-hearted angel am I."

Next, she cycles to the library to help rewrite the children's books. After all, she thinks disdainfully, *they can read about me if they can read about witches, goblins and crooks.*

Much to the children's delight, she's off to the zoo to tell the animals that they can talk back to the children if they feel inclined to.

The children let out groans, and sucking on her lollipop, she says, "Well, time for me to go," and with a cheerful wave, she's on her way…

To create havoc back in heaven and not just for a day.

In memory of my big brother David, you always believed heaven was full of love and laughter, I know it is, because you are there.

I Wanted to Run but She Made Me Crawl

Sheets of rain fell unceasingly as Jeff sat huddled on a park bench, almost in a foetal position. The park was deserted due to the weather, and Jeff thought miserably that if any onlooker passed by him, he would look like a right idiot, soaked to the skin, his tears mingling with the rain. But he didn't care. In the state he was in, both mentally and physically, inflicted by the punches, kicks and bites from Liz, today, he just didn't care.

He buried his head in his shaking hands and knew with utmost clarity that it was over between him and Liz; he just could not cope anymore. Vivid memories of the horrors of today would haunt him for a long time. He realised that whilst the physical scars would disappear with time, the psychological scars would be with him forever.

The lines from the band U2's *Sweetest Thing* kept playing in his head, "My love she throws me like a rubber ball – she won't catch me or break my fall." The memories came thick and fast, flashing back to the first time he had ever met Liz.

He was staying in a flat with his sister Susan, an avid reader. Every time you see her, she had her nose stuck in a book, Jeff thought. She was in bed with the flu and handing Jeff a list of books she wanted to read, asking him to go to the local library and see what he could borrow. A disgruntled Jeff made his way to the library with the slip of paper in his hand, thinking, *If after ten minutes of scouting shelves, I can't find the authors that she wants, I'll just pick up any old books.* He was playing football with his mates later that day and wanted to get some goalie practices in.

And then he saw her; the librarian was stamping books behind the desk. He looked at her and looked again. *God, she's a right cracker*, he thought – long black hair, bright blue eyes and a small elfin face. She glanced up at him and smiled, the sweetest smile he had ever seen, and he was smitten.

Jeff handed her the slip of paper with Susan's favourite authors and asked if she could help him. He remembered that she had on a multi-coloured top and figure-hugging jeans, and even though she was in flat sandals, she was slightly taller than him. He cast a quick glance at her left hand – no rings; God, just maybe he was in with a chance, and this could just be his lucky day.

The library was quiet, just a few people using the computers, so before anyone else came in looking for books, Jeff, stumbling over his words asked if she would like to grab a coffee or a drink with him after work. She smiled and said, "Yes, I'd like that," and that had been the start of a relationship, which once had been the best thing that had ever happened to him.

They had so much in common; both were keen walkers, both loved restaurants and had similar tastes in music, except that Liz hated football whilst Jeff was a football fanatic whether watching it on TV or playing for the local town team whenever he got a chance. They had loved and laughed a lot back then, Jeff recollected with a tinge of sadness.

But that's where their similarities ended. Jeff was gentle and placid and rarely lost his temper. Inciting anger in him required severe provocation. In fact, his sister Susan would often tell him he was a walk-over, too soft for his own good. When one of his mates would come on the phone asking for a loan of money until payday or to borrow his car, Jeff would just oblige and shrug her off her criticism.

Liz was the polar opposite; volatile and quick-tempered. In Jeff's eyes, Liz saw life purely in black and white; there were no shades of grey. Sometimes when meeting friends in a pub, Liz would have one too many drinks and start making hurtful comments about other people standing around them. One night, Jeff remembered, in a loud slurred voice, she had pointed over to a teenage girl who had seemingly tried a fake tan, which had failed dismally, and said, "Will you just look at the size of her, and with that colour, she's the spitting image of a Jaffa orange. What a sight!"

When such hurtful remarks started, Jeff would leave the pub, stand outside waiting for an unsteady Liz to come out and then silently walk her home. He'd learnt by this time not to stay in the pub imploring her to be quiet because then her vicious comments would rain down on him. Scathing remarks such as, "Pathetic wimp, I just put up with you because I feel sorry for you."

Attempts to stop her only seemed to fuel her anger. Often Susan would furiously comment after a night out, "Liz was a real bitch tonight. She needs to keep that big gob of hers shut, or by God, one of these days, Jeff, somebody will do it for her. She really is going to meet her match, and believe you me, she will come off the worst, and it will serve her right."

"Will you just shut up about it, Susan," Jeff said irritably, but he knew in his heart that she was absolutely right.

That's when the physical abuse began. Back at her flat after a night out, she began smashing glasses against the kitchen walls and screaming obscenities at Jeff. Then, suddenly she began slapping him again and again in the face. Jeff picked up his jacket and left the flat, putting this first and only episode of physical abuse down to Liz having too much alcohol.

Now, the only time he seemed to make her happy was when he showered her with gifts – perfume, clothes and weekend getaways to expensive hotels. He tried to keep her content and above all not answer her back, anything to keep the peace.

She had become more and more possessive, e-mailing him at work every hour, checking his mobile phone to see who had phoned him and screaming obscenities if he had played football with his mates.

One Saturday, after a game of football and a few pints later, he arrived at her flat; they were supposed to go to the cinema. He knew the second he saw her she was in one of her rages. Broken bottles, plates and glass were strewn all over the kitchen floor. She began screaming at him. "You're pathetic, sad git. You're half an hour late. Do you think your time is so precious and I've got nothing better to do than wait on the likes of you?"

Suddenly, Jeff felt the impact of a punch into his left eye.

He silently picked up his jacket and left the flat. On closing the door, one of the neighbours opened his door and gave him a look of pure contempt, and it hit Jeff harder than any punch would ever do. The neighbours were hearing all the screams, fighting and glass-smashing, and they obviously thought it was Jeff abusing Liz and not the other way around. At that moment, Jeff just wanted to curl up in a corner and not get up again.

Going to work the next day with a black eye was awful. He said he had had too much to drink and got into a fight. Tony, his boss, had looked at him incredulously, and his sister Susan, well, quite frankly, she just didn't believe him, saying, "It's that bitch you're seeing, I know it." In the end, Jeff stopped playing football and seeing his mates; it wasn't worth the pain and aggravation.

Once, Liz went away for the weekend to stay with her brother in London. He was on his own, and God, it felt good. He walked through the park carrying two tins of paint. He had promised Liz he would finish redecorating the kitchen before she came home. Then, he would sit and relax over a few cans watching football.

He walked slowly through the park, watching others enjoy the warm summer sunshine, and bought himself a huge ice cream, something he hadn't done in years.

As he walked, he realised that he still loved her when she was her old self, but the old Liz was diminishing every day. Isolation is the key to abuse, and he was becoming more isolated as Liz's abuse increased. He rarely saw his mates now and had even lied to Susan, making out that he was going around to see one of his friends when he was really just going for walks. *Enough of this self-pity*, he thought to himself; *I'm going to enjoy today, although it shouldn't be like this. I should be missing her,* and with a jolt, Jeff realised he wasn't missing her at all. He pushed these thoughts away and carried on walking.

He let himself into the flat whistling tunelessly – *God, I feel happy today,* he thought as he made his way into the kitchen, taking off his T-shirt drenched in sweat. Then he heard footsteps coming from the bedroom.

Liz walked slowly towards him, and he instantly knew it was different this time. He felt his stomach churning and his throat drying up. He tried to speak, but no words came out as he looked into her face – her face was contorted in a mixture of pure evil, loathing and anger. "You lazy, sad, sick waster. You were supposed to have finished painting the kitchen," she hissed, lashing out at him, punching, scratching and biting him. She turned around and picked up the boiling kettle, and he knew this time that she wasn't going to throw it at the walls. He ran from the flat and kept running.

Sitting on the park bench, he felt like a broken man, a shadow of his former self constantly living in fear, too ashamed to admit to his sister, his mates and his work colleagues about being abused. He had tried to keep it hidden; after all, it was women who got abused, wasn't it?

There was no going back now. He knew that once Liz's temper was under control, his mobile phone would start ringing. It always did. She would say how much she loved him, and she would change, but this time, he finally faced the truth. She would always be this way, and if it wasn't Jeff suffering, it would be someone else.

He was one of the lucky ones – how many men and women suffered in silence for the sake of the kids, due to lack of money or having nowhere else to go, or because they had become so used to being abused it had begun to fit into what was "normal" everyday life?

Jeff slowly left the park knowing that in time, the physical scars would heal and disappear, but how long the mental scars would take, he didn't know.

A Cool Time

Laying in a bubble bath and slowly sipping a glass of Chardonnay, for once, Delia felt perfectly relaxed. In appreciation, she looked around her bathroom, painted aqua blue – the colour of the sea on a summer's day. The tiny gold-rimmed ceiling lights were dimmed gently to show off the multitude of flickering candles surrounding her bathroom. This room was large compared with the rest of the rooms in the house. Her dad was a joiner by trade, and he had excelled himself in revamping the bathroom. The walls were adorned with prints of her favourite paintings, such as by Winifred Owen, Monet and Jack Vettriano, as well as framed pictures of her laddies, each one telling a tale of their childhood. Some coloured, others black-and-white. Delia knew it would seem strange to others, but this was her favourite room in the house, full of sentimental knick-knacks. She knew that for most people, the kitchen was the heart of the home, but not for her. She closed her eyes and listened to soft, soothing music, which was a mixture of soft rustling trees and the gentle swoosh of waves crashing on the shore.

As Delia took another sip of the wine, she smiled, but by

God, she had not been smiling at 5 am this morning. Her sons Max and Roy who just turned fifteen and thirteen were going on a school camping trip for a long weekend, and for the last two days, she had been on at them to pack whatever paraphernalia they needed. At first, she had tried to coax them to get their act into gear, and it was met with the usual response: "In a minute, mam" or "I'm busy" – *like they had so many other more important tasks to complete*, Delia thought resentfully. Well, just wait until they've landed at some godforsaken campsite and got soaked to the skin; their mobile phones wouldn't keep them warm, that was for sure, but all they had harped on about was reminding each other not to forget their phones. In the end, it had ended almost in a screaming match – on her part anyway. It was Max's last few remarks that had just about finished her off. Deliberately, patiently, with his arm leaning on the kitchen table, he had said, "Mam, we will not miss the school bus, so will you just calm down," knowing full well that saying that was like showing a red rag to a bull. Delia, who detested the phrase "calm down," shouted at them furiously, "I've spent the last two days washing all your filthy clothes so you both could look presentable, and the least you two can do is put them in your rucksacks. Max, get up into that loft and get down the sleeping bags, and Roy, you collect your sandwiches from the kitchen."

"What's on the sandwiches?" Roy asked suspiciously.

"Tuna," she snapped.

"Oh, well," he said with an air of resignation, "I suppose that will have to do us, but I thought maybe a nice bit of roast beef and some homemade chocolate cake wouldn't go amiss," he added, a picture of innocence. Max sniggered; now the pair of them were taking the mickey out of her, instead of goading each other, for a change.

"Well, Mam," Roy laughed, "You might be called Delia, but you're no Delia Smith, are you?"

Both of them now doubled up, laughing at Roy's joke. Delia decided to ignore this last remark, well aware she was not renowned for her culinary expertise.

"Aye, she might not be Delia Smith, but I think she's in the same league as Judge Judy," Max sniggered. The laddies were laughing so much now that Delia could not help but join in.

Finally, the boys were about to be on their way, and after a quick cuddle, Delia closed and locked the front door. She lifted her eyes to the heavens and whispered to God, "Take care of them, and thank you for a few days of peace."

She padded into her freshly-painted, sunshine-yellow kitchen, frowning at the pile of breakfast clutter. Then knowing once the kitchen was cleaned up, there would be no one except herself to mess it up, she made herself a mug of coffee and, armed with a notepad and pen, began to make a list of all the things she would like do now that she was on her own. Not a list of what she should be doing – if she were to do that, she would be in her dotage. She knew she wouldn't get around to doing half the things she had written, but it made her feel like she was being positive and optimistic.

1. Go to the museum, art gallery and library.

2. Weather permitting, pack a picnic and have a lazy afternoon on the beach.

3. Sit outside my favourite Italian restaurant with a glass of wine and watch the world go by.

4. Stroll around the local market.

5. Pamper myself, i.e. go for a much-needed haircut.

6. Make a surprise meal for dad – okay, ready meal and dessert.

As Delia looked out of the kitchen window, she could see the sun was already rising. It was going to be another glorious Indian summer's day, and she was not going to waste a minute of it. She quickly slipped into her favourite knee-length dress, white and covered in tiny, red poppies She then wore white sandals and tied her long auburn hair into a plait. Making sure she had her purse, lipstick and sunglasses, she locked the front door and made her way along the cobbled streets to the outdoor market. She felt like a child, like when she used to have a day off school, pretending to be ill, when Mam would be so sick to the back of her teeth that she would tell her to outside to play. At the market, she bought a few scented candles, a bag of assorted sweets for the laddies and pan drops for her dad, his favourite. She enjoyed the stroll and listening to the banter of the people around her.

It was almost lunchtime as she slowly made her way past the tourist shops and cafes to the art gallery, spending a happy hour admiring many of the paintings and shaking her head in disbelief at others – *how could some of these be called art?*

The gallery had a whole room devoted to unwrapped toilet rolls that hung from the ceiling.

"My God," she said, not realising she was talking out loud, "What a total waste of toilet paper."

She swung around as a voice behind said laughingly, "I completely agree with you. It's just I was too afraid to say it out loud in case the so-called artist was in the vicinity."

Delia blushed crimson, brought a hand to her mouth and

whispered, "It's not you, is it, the artist, I mean?"

He began to laugh so hard that Delia said irritably, "It's not that funny."

He laughed again and said mockingly, "Actually, I believe a four-year-old could have done better than this."

Delia now smiled at the elderly man with thick white hair, twinkling blue watery eyes and a strong Irish brogue. Even in old age, he was still handsome; he must have been a stunner when he was young, Delia surmised. His name was Daniel. Although frail, he was dressed immaculately in a black suit, white shirt and green tie, leaning on a walking stick. Delia was conscious of his fragility as they walked slowly together through the art gallery, arguing about certain paintings, whispering and laughing together at other so-called works of art. Finally, they had a drink together at Daniel's favourite Irish pub, wine for her, Guinness for him. He was a good soul, she thought, lonely just like her dad. Her instincts told her that Daniel and her dad would have much in common. Both their wives were dead, and they shared an Irish ancestry. Perhaps in time, they would become good friends.

Delia had invited Daniel to come for a meal to meet her dad. Mum's death had left a huge void in his life. Okay, maybe she was meddling, but there were so many lonely people in this world; perhaps they could provide company for each other.

She was cooking them both a special meal – well, a Marks and Spencer ready-to-serve meal. Pork cooked in mustard and cream, roasted potatoes, glazed carrots with rhubarb crumble and clotted cream for dessert. Thank God for ready-made meals, she thought.

GARDEN IN HEAVEN

She knew Dad wasn't too keen on her lack of culinary skills although he never said a word in case he hurt her feelings. But tonight, she couldn't go wrong, all she had to do was heat it up, and if she set the table with candles and soft lights, it should go wonderfully. Cans of Guinness for Daniel, a bottle of Glenmorangie for Dad and wine for herself.

She sipped the last of her wine and decided to make herself presentable for her guests when her mobile rang. It was the laddies saying they were having a "cool" time.

She laughed inside her head at the words "cool" and told them that she was having a "cool time too". As she thought about her day and looked forward to the evening, she realised, in surprise, that she was actually having "a cool time."

Our Day

I sit in a cove and watch the sun rise, turning the dark sea into a glittering carpet of silver and gold.

I wait for you to find me. I know you will, and as you walk towards me, we smile. That same smile we have for each other – still.

You reach for my hand and we walk barefoot and carefree across the golden sand.

We laugh and play like the children we used to be, and as we lie on our favourite sand dune, we talk of our wishes and dreams and of a future that is still to be.

We go collecting rare and colourful shells, dipping our toes in the sea. No one is there; only you, only me.

In the darkness, we climb to the top of our garden and look at the scene around us. Thousands of stars envelop us as we look towards the sea. We listen to the sound of breaking waves and the rustling of wind blowing gently through the trees.

Today was our day – a day for only you, only me.

Printed in Great Britain
by Amazon